About the author

One of seven, always playing sport as a kid. When married, I used to keep diaries. In family cards, I'd write poems, or a little story to the recipient.

My work for many years was in the transport industry, then the Port of Dover. My jobs were administrative, so I wrote many, many reports, completing endless documentation. Luckily, I like writing!

More recently, I delivered the mail, progressing to the role of a postman! Having experienced many challenges, mistakes and changes in recent years, I'm an easy going, laid-back, happy father.

Plus, wonderfully, I'm a grandad... and now, an AUTHOR!

LAURA, COME BACK TO ME

Michael Dowle

LAURA, COME BACK TO ME

Vanguard Press

A CIP catalogue record for this title is
available from the British Library.

ISBN 978 1 784653 75 0

*Vanguard Press is an imprint of
Pegasus Elliot MacKenzie Publishers Ltd.*
www.pegasuspublishers.com

First Published in 2018

**Vanguard Press
Sheraton House Castle Park
Cambridge England**

Printed & Bound in Great Britain

Dedication

This book is dedicated to my mum. She loves reading. It's taken a while, but number four has finally achieved his dream.

Can you believe it Mum, we've got an author in the family!

Acknowledgements

To all of the following, I'd like to say thank you for your input, and listening to me rambling on. I'm sure I bored you all senseless!

My family: Rich and Maureen, Jeannie, Kate, Barbara, my grown up kids, plus Vera and Beverley.

And those I call friends: Gary and Bev, Shirley, Jamie and Jane, Margaret and Jim, John H, Danny Wallop, and finally Roz.

1. It started when we said hello

Now, at just twenty-five years old, sitting on the sofa in the flat we shared and lived in, I was still in denial; it was just four days after she'd died.

It was now January the ninth, 2014.

Here in Broadstairs, on the east coast of Kent, its windy enough most days of the year, except some summer days, and even those can be breezy. But wintry days like this often have, along with the wind, a biting cold which comes in from the sea and never leaves the seaside town alone.

Yet another day had passed and I'd gone through the motions of life running our own antique shop on autopilot mode. It seemed pointless being there now without her.

Outside, through the living room window, I saw there was still snow on the ground, with the sea beyond the deserted beach, merging as one with the greyness of the sky on Viking Bay. Over on the north of the bay, perched near the edge of a rocky cliff, was Fort House, where Dickens had spent many summers in the mid-nineteenth century, writing as he'd looked out to sea.

'This wasn't supposed to happen! We were soul mates, Laura!' I shouted out to nobody but myself. Tears were in my eyes once again.

Weary with emotion, I found myself with my head in my hands, remembering the day we'd first met...

It was 2004. Almost ten years ago, when I was sixteen years old.

I was in Laura's father's shop, which exploited the Dickensian connection as so many Broadstairs shops and restaurants do—it was called *The Old Curiosity Shop*. It was situated in one of those narrow Victorian side streets hidden behind Viking Bay, which wasn't far from the small cottage where I lived then, with my mother and younger brother, Harry.

I'd always been crazy about antiques ever since I could remember, and I recalled the time when my mother allowed me into the small parlour room she used downstairs in our cottage home, to pick an item for myself to keep and look after on that day in 2004, my sixteenth birthday, the twenty-sixth of June. Though there was no way Mum could have owned or afforded a shop, she was deeply interested in antiquities, so that must have been where I gained my interest, or so I always believed.

She had a collection of odd and strange antiques herself back then, such as an Anglo-Saxon shield and spears, along with figurines of ancient silver soldiers from that era. Also, she had some old flints and three stones, which she said, more than once, were from the really olden days, dating back to the Neolithic age, apparently being of special importance to us all. "There are only four such stones in existence," she'd say. Three belonged to her and the fourth was with an old cousin of hers, so she believed.

But the treasures that interested me were her small Indian statues, silver and gold goblets, watches, glass bowls, fruit bowls, silver spoons, and Irish ceramic gnomes. I had more interest in items that were smaller, rather than larger.

Finally, I picked a Japanese presentation bowl which was full of colours, decorative flowers, and leaves adorning its outer edge, which Mum explained to me was more than one hundred years old. She said in her ever-comforting, lovely, soft Irish voice that it'd stay in the parlour, but it was now mine forever. I promised to take care of it always.

We never had much money, and since dad had passed away when I was ten and my brother Harry was just nine years old, things had been tough for us all. Dad was a tall man with dark brown hair and a strong Irish accent. Mum said he was a handsome man and great fun, always making us laugh, and he was a happy soul. We all missed him terribly, Mum especially so.

I remembered then that Dad used to say that Mum was gorgeous, and they were always cuddling each other. She had short black hair with occasional dyed gold and sometimes green streaks, which showed she was different, I always thought. Plus, it defined and denoted hers (and our) Irish heritage. We'd moved to this area on the Kent coast of England when Harry and I were small boys, from Ireland, to start a new life. Mum was about five feet six inches tall, her blue eyes darker than mine, with a soft, but strong, Irish accent. There was always a happy smile on her face. Working regularly as a cleaner, she also read people's palms and tarot cards, making herbal tea for many of the locals when they visited our cottage, and was very well respected by the towns-folk. They always greeted her kindly, most stopping at length to talk to her.

Maybe it was because of her warm manner that people liked her so much, though I'm sure that her Irish origins and friendliness came from her upbringing, back in Ireland.

She supported us with her palmistry, fortune-telling and cleaning work. Sometimes people would come to our small cottage, visiting the downstairs parlour room. We weren't allowed to go in there, other than the time she gave me my birthday present; although, Harry and I used to sneak in without her knowing, when she was out at work. I knew that there were old reading books on a dusty shelf and cabinet in there, plus her tarot cards and herbs, though we weren't allowed to eat the herbs as they were inedible!

The herbs were all in small glass jars labelled with different names, which then I did not fully understand. One jar in particular had a label on it saying 'dried stinging nettles'. I couldn't understand why anyone would want to use such herbs and just get stung! Mum read people's palms in that room, and used the herbs for making different tea to drink before telling their fortunes, through the leaves left in the cups once they'd drank the tea.

But people didn't come to the parlour room very often. If someone did come, or maybe if a couple came, it would be two or three weeks before they came again, and so she went out cleaning. Her activities in this respect even reached the exalted height of Bleak

House, which Mum would go and clean pretty thoroughly about once a fortnight.

However, though there never seemed a lot of money back then, we didn't go hungry. One of the wonderful things about her was that she'd make a meal for Harry and me with next to nothing. Often, she'd say to me, 'Okay, tell me, Jack,' in her soft Irish voice, 'what've we got in the cupboards and fridge?'

'Well, we've potatoes here and some mincemeat,' I would reply.

'You know what that means, Jack?'

'What Mum? What?' I'd say, knowing what her reply would be.

'It's your favourite for sure, meat and potato pie!' she would say, getting as excited as me.

I loved Mum's cooking, and that meal was our favourite. On that particular birthday, she managed, somehow, to give me ten pounds.

So it was, on that sixteenth birthday, I knew what I wanted to do when she gave me the money. My interest had already been awakened by the strange things Mum kept in the parlour, especially as I'd been to *The Old Curiosity Shop* to look at small antiques myself, but I had never met Laura before, only her father. Indeed, I had not realised I had known of her existence until that actual birthday.

'Mum,' I said. 'I'm going out.'

'To meet some friends on your birthday, son?'

'No, I'm going to *The Old Curiosity Shop*.'

'And what is it you'll be doing there?'

'I'm going to have a look around, hope to buy an antique of my own with my birthday money, to go alongside my new Japanese fruit bowl you gave me.'

'Oh Jack, bless you. Your brother Harry can stay with me and help me prepare tea later. Well, you may not find anything there for ten pounds, but have a look anyway. Dempsey is a good man. Tell him I said hello, son, I've not seen him for a while now.'

'Okay, I'll tell him you said hello and I'll have a good try to find something for my little collection of antiques, too,' I said as I made my way out of the cottage, kissing her on the cheek goodbye.

Walking to the shop, I had a big smile on my face, feeling proud to be going out to shop for an antique that would be truly mine.

When I arrived, I looked up at the sign above the shop, *The Old Curiosity Shop*, one proprietor Mr Arthur Dempsey named on it. As I walked in, I heard the ding-a-ling bell that meant a customer—myself—was in the shop.

As soon as I was inside, the door closed itself behind me, and I gazed around at the many items of old furniture, glassware, silverware, watches, and all manner of varying antiquities. The sight of these treasures momentarily took my breath away and, feeling excited and slightly light-headed, I looked around in amazement at everything there. But, more than the view, I realised that the dizziness was caused by something else: a pleasant odour of perfume, coming from the direction of the shop counter. I could see exactly where and whom that smell was coming from. I felt drawn towards it, although I could only see her outline in the dim light of the shop interior.

Glancing around, I saw that there was nobody else in the shop, other than a girl who looked possibly about my age standing beside the old wooden counter, who I thought, I'd never seen before.

She was wearing a dark green sleeveless dress with big yellow flowers all over it, which seemed a bit too big for her, as it reached from her neck down to her ankles. I could see that beneath this she wore black boots as well. Approaching her, I could see that she was nearly as tall as me. Mum always said I was tall for my age at five feet ten already. The girl had long, jet black hair and pale, slim arms. But most of all, I had felt her eyes were staring at me from the moment I'd walked into the shop. Those eyes, which I could now see as I walked closer to her, were a shiny emerald green. I liked her immediately, especially her face and those eyes.

'Hello, I'm looking for an antique at around ten pounds, if you have any. May I have a look around?' I asked nervously as I reached the counter, while she moved from beside it to behind it.

She looked me directly in the eyes, and I could feel redness creeping into my face when she replied in a deep, soft, low and confident Irish voice—slightly deeper in tone than my mother's—which surprised me. 'Hello. Yes, have a look around if you like. My name's Laura. I'm in charge of the shop. My dad isn't working today, he's gone to an antique sale this afternoon. Not a lot here for your money. Let's see if we can sort something out for you. What's your name?'

'Jack,' I said, still very nervous. 'Jack Stanton. And today's my birthday. Nice to meet you, er, Laura.'

'Well, a happy birthday to you Mr Stanton, nice to meet you, too. Tell you what Jack, have a look around the shop, okay?' she said, with a beaming smile immediately after she'd spoken.

'Thanks,' I said. 'Thanks very much.' I turned away from her, knowing my face was flushing even more, but thinking to myself that she had a wonderful smile.

So, I walked around the shop for a few minutes, strangely sensing her eyes following me as I wandered around. The shop remained empty other than us. I glanced at her once, seeing that she was still looking in my direction. We both smiled nervously at each other, I remembered. I could feel tears welling up in my eyes as I recalled that first meeting.

Finally, after looking at several small stuffed animals, silver candlesticks, goblets, pocket watches, fruit bowls, dishes, and all manner of items, I picked something to my liking. It was a small white fruit bowl, with the name Belleek, Ireland, on it. I knew it was good because Mum had mentioned this name Belleek to me before, as it was well renowned in Ireland. Plus, I'd seen similar items in one of her books, as well as knowing there was a bowl although larger than this one, in our own kitchen.

'Okay,' I said, walking back to her at the old wooden counter, with my red cheeks not feeling as hot as earlier. 'How much is that one, please, it's got no price on it?' I enquired, as I turned and pointed to the bowl, which was sitting in the front window with several other bowls.

'Hmmm, I think that's probably about ten pounds to you, sir!' she said in a light-hearted way, smiling again as she did so.

'Great. I'll take that. Thanks, er, Laura.' I said, smiling back at her.

Then, she walked straight past me from the counter to the shop front, picking up the bowl. I was again aware of her perfume as she walked closely past me, strangely feeling more comfortable talking to her now. She returned to the counter.

Passing over the ten pounds, I felt the touch of her hand, as she did mine, for the first time. We stared into each other's eyes, not knowing quite what to say, simultaneously smiling at each other yet again. I knew then that as well as liking her smile and eyes, I was beginning to really like her.

We stared at each other for those moments, and she looked away after a few seconds to get some brown paper from under the counter, to wrap up my purchase safely for me, handing over the small package, our eyes meeting once again.

'Thanks,' said Laura, breaking our momentary silence and eye contact again, as her attention moved to the clock above the shop door.

'Thank you,' I replied, knowing I was still slightly stammering my words.

'Well, it's time for me to close the shop, I'm afraid, so if you'd like to follow me?'

'Oh, sure. No problem, thanks for your help with this,' I said, raising the bowl in my hand, feeling a little more confident now.

'That's quite alright, Jack,' she said, as she led the way towards the front door of the shop, turning to smile at me again, with me now overcoming the redness and embarrassment in my face somewhat.

'I'll be back again, I love your shop and antiques.' I said to her.

'I would hope so, too, seems like we both love antiques. But not tomorrow, it's Sunday and we're closed. Bye for now, Jack.'

'Oh, I see. Well, another day then.'

'That'd be really nice. Looking forward to it already,' she said, with a little laugh. After she had spoken, I walked out of the shop.

Then she closed the door behind me, and I turned away with my birthday present clutched in my hand.

Walking home that afternoon with the bowl wrapped up by Laura in brown paper, I felt excited and happy, more so than ever before, knowing that I wanted to see her again, hoping that she felt the same way, not knowing then what was to come. And I'd got a present all of my own.

Returning home after walking through the town, I showed my mother the purchase.

'Well, Jack, I think you'd better put that with your other present I gave you earlier today, don't you think?' she said.

'Yep, good idea.'

'I think this fruit bowl you've bought is lovely, son. And it only cost you ten pounds? You may have an eye for antiques yourself, m'boy! I think it's worth much more than that.'

'Runs in the family then, Mum, don't you think?'

We both laughed then. We often made fun of each other's accents, as Mum had always kept her strong Irish accent, much more so than I had.

'Hmm. Maybe it does. I know how clumsy you can be, so I'll put this away for safekeeping in the parlour with your other Japanese bowl, if that's okay with you?'

I laughed. 'That'd be nice Mum, thanks. Oh, and by the way, in *The Old Curiosity Shop*, I met a girl who worked there and her name's Laura. Laura Dempsey. Mum, she was really nice and likes antiques like me. I don't think I've ever seen her before, apart from maybe walking home from school. Did you know about her, as you'd not seen her father Mr Dempsey for some time?'

'Yes. I knew Dempsey had a daughter. He used to visit occasionally, and she came with him a couple of times, when you were out with friends. That's why you've not actually met her before. Well, maybe you ought to ask her if she'd like to come for tea one day, it might be nice to get to know her if you like her, don't you think?'

'Yep. That's a great idea. I'll go there again next week and ask her. I think she liked me, Mum, and I think she's about my age. It felt strange meeting her. But a nice strange, you know? And she had a nice accent like yours, so I think they're Irish, or at least from Ireland like us.'

'They are. Sounds as if you do like her, Jack? You never know when you might see her again. But it'd be a good idea to get to know her, especially as you both seem to really like antiques.'

'Okay, Mum. I'll go to the shop and ask her next week.'

And later on that evening as we all sat down to have tea in the living room—our favourite meat and potato pie for my birthday—there was a knock at the front door.

'I'll get the door,' I said to Mum.

When I reached and opened it, standing in front of me I saw a stocky man, slightly taller than myself, with a moustache, dressed in a suit, wearing glasses. I recognised him from my visits to his shop. It was Mr Dempsey. And next to him, to my amazement, was Laura!

'Hello again, Jack,' she said. 'I think I've made a bit of a mistake in the shop today, d'you think my father and I could come in to talk about it?' she said in a quicker, more excited voice than earlier in the shop that afternoon.

She'd spoken to me before her father had had a chance to even open his mouth.

I was confused, but right behind me, from nowhere, my mother appeared, speaking before I had a chance to.

'Do come in. You must be Laura. I remember you from a few years ago, when you visited with your father. Hello again Arthur, it's been some time since we last met. I've already been told about you, Laura, by my son Jack, how you sold him his small fruit bowl today, on his birthday. That was lovely. Would you like some tea, we're about to eat ourselves? There's enough for us all if you so wish?'

Laura said, 'Yes please,' even before her father had tried to speak.

Standing in the doorway in front of me now, Mum turned to me as Laura stepped inside the cottage.

'Jack, would you like to make Laura a cup of tea first?'

'That'd be nice. Thank you, Mrs Stanton,' she said, whilst looking directly into my eyes once again. She reached out confidently for my hand in the doorway to our home, and I took it gently in mine, leading her into our kitchen open-mouthed, via the hallway, with my face slightly reddening again with surprise and happiness.

Behind us, I could hear the front door to our cottage closing, as we both stood in the doorway of the living room, still holding each other's hands. Turning, I heard Mum say to Laura's father, 'Come in Mr Dempsey, we don't bite y'know!' She continued, 'Now go down those few steps there and into the parlour, Mr Dempsey, so that we adults can discuss today's misunderstanding for sure.'

As we watched, Mum followed Laura's father into the parlour. She looked at us both and winked, whispering as she did, so that he couldn't hear her. 'I've known your dad for a while, Laura. Leave this to me, I'll sort it out.' Then she smiled at us and went into the parlour and closed the door.

Her father never had chance to say a word, and was open-mouthed like me. We heard him say, 'Please, Mrs Stanton, Mary. Call me Dempsey, everybody does.'

We both turned again to look at each other, smiling, then laughing. I looked into Laura's bright green eyes, getting a strange feeling in the pit of my stomach, whilst also feeling heat flushing into my face. I'd never felt like this before. It was like having a butterfly dancing around in my stomach. But, I knew then that I liked it.

Laura smiled and said, 'Come on then, Jack, cup of tea. Or would you like to show me around this grand little cottage you live in? But no tricks though!' She laughed again, and tightened her grip on my hand, squeezing gently, which felt so nice, before letting go completely.

Continuing, she said in her soft Irish voice, as she put her other hand onto my reddening cheek, 'Jack, I think you're nice. Sorry for embarrassing you. I only did that because I like you.'

Staring at her again, I didn't know what to say for a few moments. As she let her hand drop from my face and hot cheek, I felt a calmness come over me and replied, 'Er, thanks. I like you too. So, er, would you like to have a look at the cottage, then have a cuppa in a while?'

'Yes, that'd be lovely. Thanks, Jack. Show me around please,' she replied, more quietly than before.

I recalled now that she was very confident even then as a sixteen year old girl. Even now, I thought how unusual that was.

So, I showed her around our kitchen and living room, where my brother Harry was sitting eating his tea.

As he turned to look up from his meal I said, 'Harry, this is Laura. Her dad owns the shop I went to today, in town.'

'Hello, my name's Harry. This is our favourite meal.'

We both laughed, and Harry turned back to eat his meal, more interested in his food than meeting Laura.

'Nice to meet you, Harry. D'you like school?'

'Actually, yes, I do, Laura. Very much, thanks.'

'Good for you, Harry. I like school too, but can't wait to leave.'

Still eating his meal, he replied, 'Well, I think education is great for the brain. I like to study astronomy, don't I, Jack?'

'True, you do, little brother. Nice to have an interest. You like that and I like antiques. Right, we're going to have a wander about, Harry, be back in a while.'

'Okay,' said Harry, continuing to eat his dinner, not even looking up at us.

Turning to Laura, I whispered as we walked away, 'Harry's really clever y'know. Well, I think so. Much more so than me.'

'Well, I don't know about that, but yep, he seems nice, Jack. You know I like antiques just like you, don't you?'

We strolled into the kitchen. I didn't answer as we wandered around looking at some of the things we had on the shelves, before she spoke again.

'I see your mother likes old antique fruit bowls like you, Jack. Those ones in that display cupboard are like the one you bought today, only bigger. Hmm, and your mother seems really nice, too.'

'Yep, it runs in the family I think. Well the antiques interest, I mean. Mum's got lots of ornaments in the parlour, where she's gone downstairs with your dad.'

'We really do have things in common, don't we?'

'You're not wrong there, Laura,' I said, more confidently.

Finally, after staring at each other again, I turned away to lead us further around the kitchen, finally reaching the back door, which I opened to let her see our garden, but also to try and cool down my red face.

'Want to listen to some music or watch TV? I don't have a computer yet I'm afraid. We can wait for our parents to sort things out,' I said.

'Well, I like music, but I can see you've got a nice garden out there.'

I took a deep breath before speaking again. 'Would you like to see the garden, then? We've apple trees here, and flowers, plus a hidden area with a quiet walkway, too.'

'Well, our parents are chatting away, so that'd be nice,' she said, nodding her head in agreement.

Then, she grabbed my hand and pulled hard, jerking it almost out of its socket, saying to me, 'Lead the way, sir!'

'Okay,' I replied, pulling on her hand and arm just the same, but not as hard as she did to me, for fear of hurting her. We both laughed, smiling again afterwards, and I thought to myself once more how confident she was.

Laura squeezed my hand, turning towards me again, smiling an even bigger smile than before. I could feel my heart beating faster than it had ever done with excitement.

We continued then to walk, hand in hand, into the garden, a warm happy feeling inside my body I'd not felt before, with that butterfly feeling there again.

Then, strolling around the garden, I said with eager excitement in my voice, 'Look, the apple trees, bushes, and flowers are over there. And just here's the hidden area from the house, between the trees and flowers, I told you about. And our walkway out of the garden!' I had always loved our small garden at the cottage.

'Where does that walkway lead to, behind these trees?'

'To the sea and Viking Bay.'

'Come on. Let's go and walk along Viking Bay, Jack,' she said, grabbing my hand harder still.

As we walked towards the sandy beach via the walkway from our garden, she chattered away. 'I've seen you sometimes walking home from your school. Thought you looked like a nice kind of guy. Did you see me at all?'

'Well, now you mention it, I think I must've. A couple of times. Saw you with a group of friends, all giggling, after school. I walked past you on the other side of the road. Never thought you'd seen me, didn't have the courage to walk over and speak anyway. But I remember you were carrying some flowers in your hand, one time when I saw you. That's why I remember you, as that was unusual.'

'Oh. That was the day I was taking flowers to my mum's grave. She died when I was very young, but I've got some pictures Dad's always kept for me.'

'Oh, sorry. I lost my Dad when I was ten years old. I miss him.'

'Never really knew my Mum, I was only four years old when she passed away.'

'Well, we've got one parent each still, that's better than none.'

'It is, Jack.'

We walked silently for a few moments. I was thinking of my dad and how much I missed him. He had been a really happy man.

'Okay,' I said, breaking the silence, almost stumbling over as we reached the sandy beach. 'I like to walk here myself often, it's such a beautiful place, y'know?'

'I know that. I'm often walking along here myself, so how come I've never seen you walking here before, Jack?'

'Well, I usually walk here in the late evenings, sometimes after tea, and I bet you always walk along here in the daytime, earlier than me?'

'True, I do. So this'll be new for me. An early evening walk along the bay. Come on, let's go,' she said. We continued to walk along the sandy beach, with our hands hanging closely together, touching but not holding now.

'Wait!' said Laura as we reached the sea itself, 'I want to do something I hope you want to do too, Jack.'

'What's tha—' I tried to say.

But it was too late.

She had already put her arms around my neck and began kissing me firmly on my lips as we stood at the water's edge at Viking Bay.

Laura held me tightly that evening in June those ten years ago and I did the same to her. It was our first kiss of many, many more. I never ever forgot that kiss on my sixteenth birthday, and knowing that she was a mere four months older than me made no difference at all. As far as I was concerned, we were practically the same age.

I closed my eyes again right now, in present time, as I did for that first kiss, knowing how wonderful it made me feel.

Coming back to reality, I felt so, so sad, having tears in my eyes once again, knowing I'd never get to hold her in my arms ever again.

Laura wasn't here right now, as I sat alone in our flat, with moist eyes, whispering to myself, 'We never wanted to say goodbye to each other back then did we Laura, after saying hello for the first time... '

2. Early days together.

Sitting here now, four days after she'd gone, I continued to recall and daydream to myself about how quickly we had fallen in love in our early days together.

I think both of us knew we were soul mates within days of our first meeting—my sixteenth birthday—at her father's antique shop. Just a few weeks after that first kiss on the beach, when Laura and her father visited our cottage that same day, we had begun to see each other regularly. I kept that fruit bowl I'd bought that day, thanks to Mum. Whatever she said to Laura's father did the trick. I never did know, to this day, how she'd managed it, as I know now that it was worth a lot, lot more than the ten pounds I had paid for it back then.

About two months after we'd first met, I went to their house one Thursday evening to take her out. We went to different schools, with Laura at The Charles Dickens comprehensive school, and me at Dane Court Grammar, both in Broadstairs. They were large schools and although we liked them, we wanted to leave as soon as we could, at sixteen years old.

Laura and I were itching to get out into the real working world, especially, we hoped, into the world of antiques. We wanted to own and run our own antique shop. We didn't hate school, but said we'd already like to work together, so school was getting in our way.

Going to Laura's one particular evening, I had planned what I had thought would be a surprise for her.

Earlier in the day I'd sent her a text message asking if she wanted to go out that night. Arriving at her house, I knocked on the door at seven in the evening, with my own plan of action.

'Good evening, sir!' said Laura as she opened the front door to her house, almost shouting the words out to me.

'And a very good summer's evening to you too, young lady!' I replied, stopping myself from laughing, but just smiling as I said it.

'So, what've you got planned for tonight, Jack?' she said more quietly.

'Well, I thought I'd take us to the pictures. I know the local cinema's showing a film I think we'd both like to see, especially you.'

'You're teasing me, Jack, what's the movie called?'

'I'll tell you on the way.'

'All right, but for sure, make sure you do! I'll get my jacket, let Dad know, then we'll be on our way. '

'Okay then.'

'One thing though, Jack. I nearly forgot.'

'What's that?' I questioned, as she swiftly leaned forward and grabbed my jacket, pulling me towards her as she stood in the doorway of her house. Her face was almost level with mine now, as the pathway I was standing on was a few inches lower than her doorstep.

In a split second she had pulled me towards her and kissed me full on the lips. I remembered that she always loved to kiss me and often would just pull me towards her, wherever we were.

'Any idea what time we'll be finished and back home, just so I can let Dad know when I'll be back?' she said, as our lips gently parted. I could feel the heat from the slightly reddening of my cheeks. She did like to embarrass me.

'Well, it's seven o'clock now, so I reckon we'll be home by ten. The film starts at seven thirty, as its two hours long,' I said, as she placed her hand gently on my face.

'Right, okay. I'll tell Dad. Wait one sec and I'll be back. Oh, and by the way, I do know it's our two month anniversary, Jack. You'll learn I'm very good with anniversaries and suchlike,' she said, smiling at me, poking her tongue out just before she turned around.

I smiled. 'That's nice to hear. Hurry up then, or we'll be late for the movie.'

Laura grabbed her favourite dark green leather jacket from the hallway and rushed into the kitchen, telling her Dad that I was taking her to watch a film. Hurrying out of the house, putting her hand into mine, she closed the front door. Then we walked down the pathway, turning right towards the town and cinema.

Her father didn't like me calling him Mr Dempsey. He asked me to call him just 'Dempsey'. When I asked him why, the first time I'd visited their house, he explained the reason to me.

'Well, Jack. You know those old TV shows about an antique dealer called Lovejoy?'

'Yes, Mr Dempsey, of course, I like those shows.'

'There you go again, Jack. Look, Lovejoy is just plain Lovejoy and I love those shows too, so I want you to call me just "Dempsey" from now on, okay?'

'Yes, of course.'

'Yes, of course what, Jack?'

'Yes, of course, Dempsey.'

'Good, that's settled, then.'

As we walked to the cinema and I recalled that conversation with him a few weeks earlier, I hoped that he liked me and believed that he already trusted me with Laura.

She continued our conversation as we walked into town. 'So, what are you taking me to watch then, Jack?'

'You like horror movies, right?'

'Yep, you know that, we've spoken about it a couple of times. I love them, but you're not so keen, are you?'

'No, but I don't mind them, because... ' I paused. 'I've decided what to watch with you tonight.'

'Oh, you've decided, have you, Mr!' she said laughing at me.

'Well, I think you'll like it. Want to know what it is?'

'Go on then, surprise me?'

'It's called—wait for it—Dawn of the Dead.'

'Wow! I've read about it. I know the film. It's a remake from the one made in 1978. This new version is by a new director, Zack Snyder.'

'Blimey, you really do know your horror movies!'

'Sure thing. And it stars Sarah Polley and Ving Rhames. Anything else I can tell you about it?' she replied, smiling before continuing. 'Aha! Well, it's about zombies coming back from the dead, trying to take over and kill all of the normal humans in a town in the USA.'

'Hmm. Well, as you know the story, you sure you want to go and watch it?'

'Of course I do. It's a horror movie. They're my favourites.'

'C'mon then, let's get to it,' I said, as we continued to walk towards the cinema.

'You are lovely, Jack. Now, listen. I'm going to tell you something I've never told anyone else, and hope I never, ever do again, other than to you.'

'What's that?' I remembered saying back then, in genuine innocence.

Laura pulled hard on my right hand to get my attention, turning to stand right in front of me so that I had to instantly stop walking. She stood there, staring for a few seconds directly into my eyes that evening, before uttering those words to me.

'Jack Stanton, I love you.'

'You... you do? You really do?' I stammered, staring at her, both of us silent for a few moments.

'Yes. I had to tell you tonight or I would burst. I've been trying to tell you for days now, wanting to get you on your own to say it. Jack, I do love you.'

I stared at her and saw tears in her eyes, which started to run from her eyes down her cheeks. I'd never seen her cry.

But, I knew I felt the same as I stood there, still staring at her. I thought I'd known it since the first time I saw her in the shop, seeing her standing there with those beautiful green eyes.

'Wow! That's amazing. When I saw you for the first time in your dad's shop, I had a strange feeling in the pit of my stomach. Laura, I know what that was now. It's because I've wanted to tell you, too, but I've been scared you'd just laugh at me.'

'I may poke fun at you, Jack, but you've reached the real Laura Dempsey. Nobody has made me feel like this, wanted to be with me, or made me laugh, like you do. And we've talked already about getting an antique shop together. I want to be with you. I love you. Just you, as you are,' she said, still staring into my eyes, her own moist with tears, now waiting for me to reply.

'Well, I'm in love with you too, Laura Dempsey. We're young, but I just want to be with you, around you as much as I can be.'

We stood on the pavement that evening, continuing to stare into each other's eyes, with our arms wrapped around each other. That was when my embarrassment of being kissed by Laura ended.

Putting my hands to her cheeks, I gently wiped away those tears, which felt warm to the touch of my fingers. When I'd dried her face, I kissed her cheeks, then her lips. I didn't care who was watching us.

After we kissed, we just smiled at each other. I remembered that wonderful feeling right now.

Finally, I realised that other people had been walking past us, staring, in the warm August summer evening.

'C'mon, let's get to the cinema,' I said again.

'S'pose so. C'mon then, or we'll be late for the movie,' she replied, as we eased out of each other's embrace, turning to walk hand in hand towards the cinema. As we walked, we both kept glancing at each other, staring and smiling on the way, in contented silence.

After the film finished, I walked Laura home. We talked on the way, as we always did.

'Did you like the film then, Jack?'

'Not bad, actually. Really gory. Think I could probably stomach more of those with you.'

'Okay, we will. So, tell me more about your mother. I know she's got a really strong Irish accent. I remember meeting her a couple of times years ago when I was younger, when my dad visited her.'

'Mum is just Mum. You know she reads palms and reads the leaves from the teacups. Works as a cleaner, as well. Everyone likes her. Makes me and Harry laugh. Tells us stories of when she used to be in Ireland when she was younger. Used to play that Gaelic football game they still play. She was in a mixed team until she was fourteen. Then it was boys only, no girls' teams anywhere at all. So, guess what she did instead?'

'I don't know, just tell me, please?' she pleaded.

'Well, she started running. And I bet you'd never guess or know that she won the Irish ladies' marathon when she was sixteen years old, sometime in the 1970s, I think.'

'Really?'

'Yes, really. There's an old photo she keeps with her trophy somewhere, but she never mentions it to anyone.'

'Wow. And she's slim for her age, Jack. Being a woman now, you wouldn't notice things like that,' she said, raising her eyebrows and smiling at me.

'Hmm. Well, she's always been interested in antiques, like us. S'pose that's where I get it from. She told me that even now she goes walking on the coast occasionally, like she did as a girl, looking for stones and fossils.'

We both paused for a moment before she spoke again. 'And she collects antiques, like her bowls, shield, and old books that are in the parlour. I remember seeing them as a little girl.'

'True, she does. Not any average Mum, well, whatever that's supposed to be. But I don't think she's average. She's the best.'

'You're lucky, Jack. I think she's lovely. I really like your mother, she's cool.'

Continuing our walk to her house, we held hands on the way, walking silently until we arrived.

After talking about Mum, I thought to myself that I could get into the horror movies myself. That movie was pretty good, even with all the blood and body parts all over the place. And we'd got in okay, although we were underage too.

It was the night our relationship changed.

When we got to her house, I went in too, as it was a quarter to ten. Dempsey had the TV on, though he was asleep in front of it. Laura gave him a shake and a nudge when we walked into the living room, and he began to wake from his slumber.

He bade us goodnight then, thanking me for bringing Laura home before wobbling up to bed. I could see and smell that he'd been drinking.

'He'll sleep like a log now,' said Laura, as she held up a bottle of whisky that he'd obviously been drinking from.

'Will he really be okay?' I questioned.

'Fine. He has a drink now and again, talks about my mum and how much he misses her. He'll sleep it off and just have a thick head in the morning.' 'Would you like a drink? Whisky, beer, tea, coffee?' she said smiling at me waiting for my reply.

'Tea, please. Don't like the look of that whisky much.'

Walking into the kitchen, I followed Laura as she put the kettle on.

'Just going upstairs to get changed, Jack. Put the radio on. And can you make the tea for us, please? You know I have no sugar, I'm sweet enough, huh?'

'I think so, yes,' I said, smiling at her as she turned to leave the room.

I made the tea, and a few minutes later, she came back into the kitchen wearing a dressing gown she'd changed into for bed. Underneath, she had a nightie on. I remembered now, I thought back then, she looked sexy, very attractive.

'Hey, I love this record, do you know it?' she said.

'Yep, I do. It's "Our Day Will Come". That's one of my favourites.'

'Mine too, what a coincidence,' she said, then paused before continuing. 'Dad's asleep. Let's have the tea in the front room, shall we?'

I suddenly realised I'd been staring at her, open-mouthed, when she said that, thinking about the words to that song, also knowing I was having trouble controlling myself!

'Er, okay.' That was about all I could say as she turned the radio off and took off her dressing gown, leaving it in the kitchen so that I could clearly see the outline of her body, her nightie clinging to her skin.

Walking into the front room, I could feel the heat in my face rising as I heard Laura close the door behind her. I sat down on the settee, still holding the cups in my hands. Sitting next to me, she took both cups from my hands, placing them onto the table nearby. She'd always been confident, I recalled again.

'Jack,' she said, as she stared at me smiling, putting her hand on my hot face, turning it towards her, kissing me gently before continuing. 'You do want to, don't you?'

I knew exactly what she meant.

'Yes, I do, if you do?' I replied nervously.

She nodded in agreement.

We never touched our tea. Under her nightie, I could see she was naked as I slipped my hand inside it to feel her breasts and body. She felt wonderfully warm.

She helped me take my clothes off as we smiled silently at each other, about to make love for the first time...

From then on, we continued to have some great times together, not just going to the cinema but making love whenever we could. We enjoyed each other's company whatever we did. However, going to the cinema as often as possible gave us the chance to show

how much we loved each other on our return, usually at Dempsey's house.

I even grew to like the horror movies Laura liked so much. We watched different ones, such as *The Faculty*, *Bride of Chuckie* and *Carrie*. Laura knew the stories before we'd even seen them, and although some weren't brand new releases, she always read the reviews before we saw them, hiring DVDs sometimes instead of the cinema. It was me who was more scared, jumping out of my seat on several occasions when we watched them. We both liked old romantic movies, too, I think I got that from my mum, as I used to sit and watch them with her sometimes when I was young, before I met Laura.

And we spent time with Mum, who let us in the parlour room to see her books and antiques, especially as she knew our keen interest in antiques.

With her allowing us into the parlour and Dempsey having his shop, we already knew that we wanted to work in antiques, more or less from the time we met.

So it was that Dempsey—already having Laura working in his shop—decided that upon finishing school, he'd allow me to work there too.

Starting work only part-time upon leaving school at sixteen, we began to look at ways of making bigger and better profits in the shop. Laura came up with the idea of using the internet to drum up trade from all over the world. It took time to set up the computer programmes, as we used our own wages from the shop to buy the equipment. Dempsey let us use the back office behind the shop, saying he hoped it would be good for business. Fortunately, Laura was very adept with computers and their systems, proving to be a real whizz-kid!

Within a year of us starting work together in the shop, the equipment was set up and Laura had organised contacts in the United Kingdom, America, and Europe. She was amazingly organised. Whilst she did this, I began and continued travelling to London and to other antique fairs, looking for items we could make a profit on, sometimes with Laura or Dempsey.

We continued building our own little empire through Dempsey's shop, whilst hankering after our own shop one day.

So, we had many good times together. Going to occasional parties with friends, staying in working on plans for our future, or watching movies at the cinema or at our parent's places.

One of my particular favourite movies was Halloween: Resurrection. Don't know why, it just was. Laura bought it for me as a present, knowing I'd enjoy watching it with her. We both liked to keep fit, too, and even though we were young, enjoyed going to the local gym to work out. And I liked to run. Laura thought I was daft, as I'd often go running for four or five hours at a time, because one day I wanted to run a marathon, just like Mum did all of those years ago.

We'd both been fortunate enough to work in *The Old Curiosity Shop* since leaving school. I recalled what Dempsey had said a couple of years later, on Laura's eighteenth birthday, when we were in the shop.

'You two have a passion for antiques, so I want you to continue to run this shop for me, and expand it through this World Wide Web phenomena I don't fully understand. You know I'm not into technology like you both are, so see if you can make our shop popular around the world, like you're trying to do in America, maybe. I'll keep on top of the finances with your help, Jack, seeing other business people like dear old Richard Leonard in London occasionally, with you. If it works out well, you never know, I could help you to get your own shop one day.'

'Dad, that's wonderful. We'll do our best. You know we love working here.'

'Thanks, Mr Dempsey. Sorry, I mean Dempsey,' I said, absolutely blown away with the gesture back then. 'You know we won't let you down.'

'I know, Jack. I can see how much this means to you and Laura. You've been working in the shop now for two years, so I think you've proved—even at your age—this is what you both want to do. See how you go, and if this works out, I'll try and help you—like I said—get your own place eventually.'

Laura hugged her father, said thank you, then went into the back office to answer the telephone. When she did, Dempsey spoke to me quietly.

'Jack. Listen to me. She's all I've got since I lost her mother years ago. I know you two are close, but I want you to know now, that if anything happens to Laura, I'll hold you personally accountable. You understand me, don't you?' He sounded aggressive in his tone when he said this to me, even though he was whispering.

'Think so, sir. But we'll be fine, I'll always take care of her, no need to worry on that score at all.'

'Just so you know, Jack, that's all.'

'Not a problem, Dempsey. I love your daughter, always have.'

'That's as maybe. But remember what I've said. Now let's see who she's got on that phone, shall we?'

Remembering this now, I thought it a peculiar thing to say—as I did then—as if he had actually been threatening me. But on the other hand, surely he was only looking out for his only daughter? I didn't dwell on it then, especially after him saying he'd help us maybe get our own shop. He was inherently a good man, I thought, and still do.

By the time we'd both turned eighteen we had a reputation as wheeler dealers already, due to the buying and selling of items throughout the UK and Europe. We had contacts, but not as yet any sales in America, hoping that would come in time.

In the meantime, we managed to save money ourselves, wanting still to get our own shop. Laura was fiercely independent, more so than me. So, we saved and saved, but not all of the time.

I recall Mum using a phrase and saying a few times to us, 'Work all day makes Jack a dull boy.'

So, whenever she said that, it reminded me that it was time for a break. We had a holiday each year in Europe to get away from everything, as I still lived at home in the cottage, with Mum. We liked to share lazy days in the sun, but also enjoyed a stroll around local shops whenever we were abroad, in case we saw anything interesting. Harry went off to university to study astronomy, so was only around in the holiday periods.

Expanding our business over the next four years, we continued to save as much as possible. Harry, after finishing his degree, decided he wanted to be a priest. Mum, at first, was surprised. But, after speaking to him and understanding why, pointed him towards the direction of a seminary in Ireland. There were certain things linking astronomy, the stars, the afterlife, and also religion that fascinated him. So, it was a natural progression to become, eventually, a priest. Mum spoke often of our own Irish heritage. Harry felt drawn towards it for some reason. Although now I remember Mum encouraged him to go to the seminary he eventually decided upon.

With Harry going to the seminary to train and become a priest in Ireland, and Laura staying at her father's house to look after him, we continued working hard, enjoying our holidays together and our life, until her twenty-second birthday.

Her dad had known we wanted to get our own shop, but had mentioned nothing since we were both eighteen, though he knew we were saving hard to pursue our dream of our own shop.

So it was, after that further four years of hard work, with Laura's twenty-second birthday approaching in late February, we'd managed to save enough money ourselves, from working in her father's shop, to get our very own. We could afford to get a property that was on the main Broadstairs High Street. And visiting London and other antique fairs, we knew stock would not be a problem either.

The shop we'd found was in an ideal location, or so we thought, almost as good as Dempsey's. We wanted to prove to him that we could do this all by ourselves, so we were close to being in competition with Laura's father.

So, on Laura's twenty-second birthday, on a chilly evening after we'd closed the shop, we planned to go out for a quiet meal, just the two of us. But Dempsey had asked us to go to their house first, as he had a present for her.

As we went in, I saw to my surprise that my mother was there. Something strange was going on, I thought to myself. Laura looked at me with a quizzical look. Then Dempsey came into the hallway as we were taking our coats off.

'Right, okay you two. How's the day in the shop been? Good, I hope? Happy birthday again,' he said to Laura, hugging her and kissing her on the cheek.

'Er, yep. It has been a decent day, Dempsey,' I said. 'Busy, with lots of sales through the net, more orders to send out tomorrow. Laura's created a new advert, which is working well already.'

'Good, good. Now, come in, the pair of you. I've asked your mum over, Jack, I want to tell you both something.'

'Well dad, we've got something to tell you. But you go first.'

'I will. Okay then.'

'Mum, you all right?'

She just smiled at me and then Laura, a beaming happy smile, not speaking. Then she walked over to us both, hugging us as one.

I knew then that something was definitely going on, other than it being Laura's birthday.

'Listen you two. Do you recall what I said about the shop when you were eighteen?'

'Yes, Dad. Get on the World Wide Web, keep up the good work and we'll see how it goes.'

'Good memory. Well, I'll come straight to it. You know I've been popping all over the place, and to Hastings more, to get antiques for the shop. No other way to say it, other than I've bought another shop. I'm going to run it—the one in Hastings—because with your help *The Old Curiosity Shop* has been doing very well. I know you've been looking at properties yourselves, naturally. But, as I'm going to take on another shop, I don't want you as direct competition. I want you to own and run this one!'

There was a silence that seemed like minutes, but was only seconds.

'DAD!' shouted Laura. 'That's unbelievable! We were about to tell you we're going into competition with you. Now we don't have to. Is this for real?' I could hear the excitement in her voice, because she said it all so fast, we could hardly understand her.

There was another silence that seemed like minutes but was again only seconds.

'You bet it is!' shouted Mum. 'Dempsey's asked me over to get my opinion on this. I think it's wonderful,' she sounded just as excited as Laura.

'Keep all of the stock, you two. Jack, your mother and I know you want to move in together, which is probably overdue in this day and age. So, as well as the shop, you'll have the accommodation above it as well. Save the money you have for whatever you need. I know the shop needs upgrading. Plus, you'll have to get the proprietors name changed, too.'

'But how can you afford to do this? I know the sales are going well, but I didn't think we'd made that much money, that you could give us the shop?' I said.

'Jack, with your help, you know we've made a good profit. I'm prepared to take a chance on you two. I told you when you were eighteen that maybe, eventually, I could help. Now, I think I can.'

And because the shop was doing so well, he was giving it to us, to share the profits still, knowing that we'd worked so hard in promoting it all over the world via the internet, whilst keeping its old-fashioned quaintness.

So, that night, we didn't go out for our meal. We stayed in at Laura's father's house and, along with my mum, had a lovely quiet meal, discussing our future plans.

There was only one thing missing from this happy occasion. Still in Ireland, training to be a priest, was my brother Harry...

So, for the next three years, we worked really hard, building up our own antiques business and client base. Trips to London and other areas meant one of us running the shop on our own some days—although Mum helped out sometimes too—whilst either or both of us went travelling by car, or occasionally train, to check out artefacts we might be interested in. Laura built up the business really well via the internet, and it was all going fantastically well.

And then came Monday the sixth of January, 2014...

3. Proposal and then...

That morning, when we awoke in the flat above T*he Old Curiosity Shop,* four days ago now, Laura had prepared the most amazing surprise. Always up in the morning earlier than me, she'd already been up for half an hour before I got out of bed.

As well as our flat, we'd managed to save a little money to hopefully put down a deposit on a seaside house. Eventually, if we could afford it, we could move into a house away from the shop and the flat, but we needed more time to save first.

'Hey, Jack, do you want a cuppa this morning, or just some cereal before running me up to the train station? Don't forget I'm on the eight forty to St. Pancras, and you know I hate being late,' she shouted from our kitchen.

True, she was always efficient and a much better time keeper than me. As I dragged my body out of bed, I walked into the shower we had built for ourselves, in the flat above the shop.

We'd turned it into a small two bedroom flat, which had a separate entrance at the back; although we had another entrance for ourselves, via a side door at the front of the shop too. We'd also created a room for our stock in the roof space.

About to get into the shower, I shouted, 'Yep baby, a nice cuppa tea please. No cereal for me, I'll get a bite to eat after dropping you off at the station.'

'Okie-doke. But hurry up, Jack, time's a wasting.'

'Will do. Just getting in the shower.'

Little did I know then what she was about to do.

When I'd finished, dried off, and dressed, I put on my jeans, t-shirt, and jumper because it was forecast to be a really cold day. I walked from our bedroom above the shop to the kitchen, where Laura was sitting at the table.

In front of her was a cereal box, which I thought unusual as I'd said to her earlier, no cereal for me. Plus, her hands were also hidden from my view.

She was already dressed in her suit. The suit was dark blue and she always wore a suit to London, when we— or she—met clients. Professional and efficient, she always said.

'Jack, I want you to sit down. I've got something to ask you and it can't wait.'

'And I s'pose you want me to check the return train time for you, as if you don't already know it,' I replied flippantly, not aware of what was about to occur.

'No. Not that at all. Have a sip of your tea. But sit down first.' She used authority this time, so I thought something was up.

I pulled out the chair opposite her, just inside the kitchen, wondering why the cereal box was positioned in front of her. Sitting down and taking a sip of my cuppa, I raised my eyebrows, staring at Laura in an inquisitive, questioning way.

'Well, what's up?'

She put her finger to her lips and said, 'Shush.' We sat quietly for a few seconds before she spoke.

'Now listen, Jack Stanton.' Her voice sounded nervous, not like her, I thought. 'We've been living above our shop now for nearly three years. Business is going well. We work hard. There isn't much spare time for us other than Sundays, when the shop's closed. And we've got plans to save for our own house, to maybe work on, as well. So, I've got a question for you that I'm pretty sure I know the answer to, but need your confirmation. Knowing we love each other is not enough sometimes, so... '

She stopped speaking then, and moved the cereal box from where it sat in front of her on the kitchen table. As she did so, I saw there was an envelope behind it with my name on it, sitting in the Belleek bowl that I'd got for my sixteenth birthday all those years ago. We always kept that in a cupboard for safekeeping—but not this morning. The handwriting on the envelope I knew, was Laura's.

'This is for you, from me. Please read it very carefully, Jack. Your life may depend on it!' She smiled and laughed, a slightly nervous laugh, I recalled, handing the envelope to me.

Opening the letter, I read it to myself in my head. I could remember every word right now. Having the letter in my pocket, thinking it gave me a connection to her, I took it out and read it over again to myself.

Dear Jack,
You know I've loved you from almost the first moment I met you. Now, we've had almost ten years together, since we were sixteen. You are my tall, dark-haired,

handsome, blue-eyed, well-dressed man, who hates ties, but loves wearing trainers instead of shoes!

Starting to run my Dad's shop, and then running our own, I've only ever wanted to be with you. We are soul mates—always have been. Fate will keep us together.

While you are reading this letter, you know I've just said to you today, the sixth of January, that your life may depend on this. I'm saying to you, Jack Stanton, that I love you. And I want to be with you forever.

Depending on what you ask me next, after finishing reading this letter, will tell me everything I already think I know about you.

What are you doing on the twenty-fourth of January? That's just over two weeks from today.

I've arranged to close the shop already, booked a registry office, got a dress. Harry will be here. Dad will be here. Your mum will be here too, of course. And we both know the song we love, "Our Day Will Come".

If you want me forever, Jack, then all you have to do is ask me one question. You should know by now what that is, even with you being naïve and slow on the uptake! I want our day to come.

Ask me the question, Jack. xx

I drifted back, in my mind, to that moment four days ago, as I held the letter in my hand now...

After reading it, I glanced towards Laura. She had moved the cereal box off the table now, so there was only my cup of tea and the bowl between us. She was smiling, but had tears in her eyes. She looked nervous.

She'd always been confident and I'd not seen her like this often, in our time together. I smiled back at her. God, to me, she was beautiful.

Moving off my chair, I stood up, walking around the table towards her whilst holding the letter in my hand. We did not take our eyes off each other.

Approaching her, I felt extremely nervous, myself. Why? We'd been together in our flat for a few years now. But, this was the ultimate question that I'd always thought you only asked once. What if she said no? Surely not, after I had read her letter. No time like the present, I thought. She'd already almost asked me to marry her in a letter. But I knew I had to utter the words.

She was still sitting on her chair in the kitchen, with her arms resting on the table, her hands clenched tightly together. I stood now above her, as she looked up into my eyes.

Bending down, I put one knee on the floor and put my hands on top of hers. Then, I took her left hand in mine, all the while looking into her tearful eyes. I'd not planned it like this, but this was the time. I knew it.

'Laura Dempsey. You've got me. You've always had me, since that first day. God above blessed me with you. I love you with all of my heart. Of course I've got a question for you.' I stopped speaking for a few seconds to wipe my own eyes and then smiled at her, knowing I'd have difficulty asking her. 'Will you marry me?' I said, very nervously.

She looked into my eyes, both of us tearful still. I waited for a few seconds before she replied.

'Yes. Will you marry me too, Jack?'

'I will. Yes, I'll marry you.'

We both smiled at each other. No words for a few seconds. I could see the most enormous grin on her face, and I'll never forget that moment as long as I live.

I leaned towards her as she sat on her chair, and we kissed each other. It was a long, lingering kiss.

Once our lips had parted, she said to me, 'I love you, Jack Stanton.'

'And I love you, Laura Dempsey, soon to be Mrs Stanton.'

We both got up then, me from bending on one knee and her from sitting in the chair. We embraced, with even bigger grinning smiles on our faces. We continued to cry. We were so, so, happy as we held each other, kissing and hugging.

A few moments later, she said, as we still embraced, 'Oh God, Jack! I was so nervous about this. I know we're in love with each other, but this is the most massive thing I've ever wanted to do. But only with you.'

'You had me worried for a moment when I sat at the table. I wasn't sure what was really going on.'

'Sometimes you don't get it, do you, Jack? That's what I love about you. You're so innocent, naive, and wonderful.'

'Hmm. My turn to get embarrassed again I reckon,' I said, feeling a warm glow on my cheeks for the first time in years.

'Now, come on you, we've got lots of other plans and calls to make. And I've got a train to catch, before I get back tonight.'

'Okie-doke. Let me finish my tea, put my trainers on and I'll drive you to the station. Think we'd better make those calls to our parents, and Harry in Ireland, pretty quickly, don't you think?'

'Yes. C'mon then. Times-a-wasting, chop-chop, Jack. You know what I'm like with my time keeping!' We both laughed when she said this. It was funny, but it was true.

'Do I! Crikey. And I've just asked you to marry me. Now I'll have to put up with that all of my life. Huh! I must be mad!' I laughed again as I said these last few words.

'You know you love me, Jack. You know you do,' she said, her normal confidence returned.

'Yep, I do. I really do.'

Staring at her as I said this, I knew we were soul mates. We'd often said it to each other. It felt very natural to ask her to marry me, even after her letter had prompted me.

'Get your coat on, then. Got your bag and mobile phone? Don't want to be late for the train.'

She smiled at me and nodded whilst putting her coat on as we walked to the door to leave for the journey to the train station. Then she turned back towards me.

'I love you with all my heart, Jack. You know we bounce off each other. I'm so happy. Thank you for being you.'

'The feeling's mutual. Never thought I'd be with someone as beautiful as you in a million years. I'm the lucky one here. And I'll always love you, Laura Dempsey.' I knew my voice was croaky with emotion still, but I felt no embarrassment.

We hugged again and kissed. Then we smiled at each other. I felt wonderful, on an enormous high of emotion. It was a feeling that's impossible for me to forget.

As we left the flat, getting into the car, our old but ever reliable BMW, she called her father to tell him what had just happened.

'Hi, Dad. I'm just on my way to London to see Richard Leonard again. Thought I'd give you a call, to give you some news,' she said. Richard was an old antique friend, whom we'd seen many times before since taking over the shop ourselves. He'd been a long time close friend of Dempsey, and was now mine and Laura's too.

She put her mobile phone on speaker so that I could hear as I drove towards the train station.

'What's that then, Laura?' Dempsey questioned.

'Well, Dad,' she said, with excitement in her voice. 'This morning when we were up and about, Jack asked me to marry him! And I said yes!'

'Oh, that's fantastic news! Not before time either. Are you there, Jack, with Laura?'

'Yes sir, I am. Hope you approve. Sorry I didn't have time to speak to you earlier, for your approval; it was a bit of a surprise to me this morning!'

'Sounds like it. You have my blessing, of course, and congratulations. That goes for both of you. So, have you set a date at all?'

'Er, yep, we have, Dad,' Laura continued. Well, I have actually. The twenty-fourth of January, in a couple of weeks. It's the last Friday of the month, and I know you always close for that day once a month. See, you know how efficient I am, don't you!'

'Well, Jack, she really is very well organised, I can vouch for that. But I reckon you know that already young fella, don't you?'

'I certainly do. She had a plan of action this morning, and we'll tell you about it later today.'

'Okay, Jack. I'd like you to come to my house this evening; let's have a celebration. Ask your mum to come over if she can. It'd be nice to catch up with her. I've not seen her for a while now.'

'Will do. Mum's been quite busy lately, but we're going to call her in a minute, as well, to give her the good news.'

'Right then. You have a safe journey on the train, Laura. Love to you both. This is wonderful news. See you both tonight at my place.'

'Sure thing. We'll get to you at about eight o'clock, just in case I'm running late getting back from London on the train.'

'Good. Fine. Bye for now, both of you.' Then Dempsey's phone disconnected.

Laura called my mother on her mobile as I continued to drive to the train station. She always called my mum, Mother.

'Mother, is that you?'

'Yes, it's me, Laura. I was partly expecting a call from you today.'

'How did you know I'd be calling?'

'Well m'dear, you can call it a kind of sixth sense, if you like. Jack calls me most days, but I hadn't spoken to you for about a week, so I knew you'd be calling me soon. How are you both, good I hope?'

As Laura held her mobile phone up nearer to my ear, but still on speaker, she pointed at me to speak to my mum.

'Morning, Mum, you alright today?'

'Yes, all well, Jack, thank you. Are you taking Laura to the station?'

'Yep, she's off for the day to London again, I'm on speaker phone.'

'You have a safe journey, Laura. Be careful today.'

As Mum said this, we both glanced at each other for a moment, even though I was driving. I thought then that Mum had some idea of what could be happening.

'Will do, thanks, Mother.'

'Mum, got some news for you. This morning when I woke up, Laura was already dressed before me, as usual. She gave me a letter which I'll tell you about later.' I knew my voice was getting excited, so I just blurted the next words out. 'So, I asked Laura to marry me, Mum. She said YES!'

'Ah son, that's fantastic news. I'm so pleased for you two. Not before time though, eh, Laura?' I heard her laugh then.

'No. Not before time, Mrs Stanton!'

'Hey, what's going on? Have you two been planning this?'

'Well, not exactly, Jack. But we've spoken recently, and your mother knows you very well. Although I had the idea, she prompted me to sort of ask you, and of course, I hoped you'd agree,' said Laura.

'Mum, you're pretty intuitive, aren't you?'

'That's right, son. I am.'

'We're going to Dempsey's tonight Mum to celebrate, can you make it?'

'Of course I can. I'll be there whenever you say.'

'About eight o'clock, then?'

'Great. See you both then. Remember to take care today, Laura, won't you. Love to you both. It's wonderful news. I look forward to having a new Mrs Stanton in the family, and soon,' Mum said laughing.

'Thanks, Mother! Bye for now.'

As Laura cut off the phone, we arrived at the station. As I pulled over to park and drop her off, we turned to each other and said as one, 'I love you.' Then we laughed. Then we kissed. I always loved kissing Laura.

When she got out of the car, she said, 'Okay then, Mr Stanton, I want you here at the station to pick me up tonight at about seven o'clock. I'll text you the exact time I'll be arriving.'

'Okie-doke. I'll see you then. Have a good, productive day.'

'Will do, you too. See you tonight.'

Then she closed the car door and walked inside the station. As I drove off I could see her in my mirror going inside, waving to me. I stuck my hand outside the window, waving goodbye as well.

A few minutes later, I was back at *The Old Curiosity Shop*, parked up and opening up just before nine o'clock.

My own mobile phone went off as I opened the front door to the shop. It was Harry. Mum had already called him, I thought.

'Hey, Jack, I've had a call from Mum. I'm allowed a few calls a week here in the seminary. Apparently you've got some news for me? She wouldn't say what.'

'Well hello there, little brother. I was about to call you. How's Ireland? You working hard over there? Are all those other priests as good as you at their job?' I said laughing down the phone line.

'Everything's fine, Jack. But what's your news? You're avoiding the question again. C'mon, big brother.'

'About an hour ago, I asked Laura to marry me. And she said yes!'

'That's absolutely marvellous, Jack. Not before time, I hasten to add. So when's the big day?'

'Er, about three weeks from now on the twenty-fourth of January.'

'Whoah! You're not hanging about, are you?'

'Nope. She's organised it all already. You know what she's like Harry, pretty damned efficient and on the ball in all areas.'

'Well, I'd better make sure I'm home for that then. That's why I got that letter from Laura about being back with you for that weekend, she'd written not to mention anything to you. Now I understand why!'

'Oh I see. That's why she said this morning you'd be here. Like I said, she's so damned efficient. Well, you'd better be here, I want you to be my best man!'

'Really? Wow. Hey, that's great! It'll be a pleasure.'

'Great. I'll give you a call later on this evening. We're all going to Dempsey's to celebrate, and I'm just about to open up the shop now.'

'Okay, Jack. Hey, and congratulations. Well done brother. You two are made for each other. We all knew that, years ago. It's terrific news. We'll chat again tonight.'

'Will do, Harry. Bye for now.' And I cut off my mobile phone.

Seconds later, my phone rang again. Answering it, I knew it was Laura.

'Hello, Jack. I'm waiting at the station, but the train's running late, so I thought I'd call you just to tell you that I love you—again.'

'Hey, I love you too, the future Mrs Stanton.' We both laughed then, together.

'And don't forget to call your brother Harry, to give him the news.'

'Already done. He's delighted. And I asked him to be my best man and he agreed. He was the only choice I could ever have.'

'Brilliant. He's the best man we know, Jack.'

'Correct there.'

'Now, the next thing we ought to start thinking about is how we're going to manage in our lovely little flat, if we ever have a family.'

'Hey, you're not having a baby are you?'

'No, don't be silly, Jack! Not yet anyway. We'd have discussed that together. You know how I like things organised. I'm just saying that it'd be another step for us. I just want to know what you'd think about it.'

'Well, I think it's a great idea. We've been together for donkey's years now, so why not?'

'Oh Jack, I'm so pleased you feel the same way as I do. That's wonderful. Well, we'll just have to keep saving for a house, too, and who knows, we may have an addition ourselves in the future.'

'Yep, sounds lovely, Laura.'

There was a few seconds silence, I remembered, on our phone call, until Laura shouted out, 'No! No! Jack, I have to go.'

She never disconnected her phone. I listened to crackling and then shouting. Something was happening at the train station.

I held my phone close to my ear and heard another woman's voice shout, 'Help! Help!'

Then I heard Laura shouting back. 'Okay, I'll get him! There's enough time.'

Hearing more crackling on the phone, I shouted into it myself. 'Laura! Laura! What's happening?' There was no reply. I could only hear crackling.

Then I heard Laura speak really loudly again. 'It's okay, little fella, you'll be safe with me. Come on, let's go.'

I heard a quiet voice crying, which may have been a small boy's. No words were said, but I could hear crying and moaning.

'Laura! What's going on? Are you okay?' I shouted down my phone.

Then I heard what seemed like a bang and then silence. Fear and dread gripped me as I stared at the phone in my hand. I knew something was wrong, badly wrong.

Quickly, I grabbed my keys from the counter in the shop. I knew something bad had happened, I could sense it. I'd heard it in the voices, especially the other woman's voice shouting for help.

Locking the shop, I jumped straight into the car, driving too fast and over the speed limit. I was getting worried now.

Arriving at the station, I parked right outside, in the taxi rank. It was the nearest point to the entrance. Jumping out of the car, I ran through the doors, shoving them open with both hands, racing through them. I knew Laura's train was going from platform one. The train was there still. It must've been running late, like she'd said. I turned to my left as I got onto the platform to see a commotion about thirty feet away. There was a crowd of people standing over someone...

I raced up to the crowd, not wanting to see what I thought I would. I pushed past three men, and a woman holding a small boy's hand, and saw another man leaning over a woman lying on the floor.

It was Laura!

She had blood coming out of her mouth. A guard was trying to talk to her with his hand behind her head. 'It'll be okay, miss. An ambulance is on its way.'

I couldn't believe what I was seeing. This couldn't be happening.

I pushed the guard out of the way. I leant down and put my hand behind her head as I knelt over her. 'Her name's Laura. We're getting married in a couple of weeks,' I shouted, turning my head up towards the crowd. 'Laura, stay with me!' I said quietly, as I turned back to look at her face, holding her with both arms now, cradling her gently, feeling her shallow breathing.

They all stared at me silently.

And then the guard said to me, 'She went onto the track to save this boy's life.' He pointed in the direction of the boy, standing holding the older lady's hand. 'He'd wandered onto the track. The train came too quickly for her to get off the line herself, and she caught a glancing blow from the train. It was an accident, but she saved the boy.'

I stared at him. Then I looked back at Laura. She blinked at me as I put my face close to hers. 'Laura, can you hear me? I heard what was happening on your phone. I got here as fast as I could. You can't leave me now, not after this morning. We're getting married, remember? Laura, stay with me. Please!' I whispered and pleaded to her as I cradled her in my arms.

'Jack. I'm sorry,' she whispered back to me. Then she smiled at me while I gently held her in my arms, still leaning over her. The trickle of blood from her mouth stopped. She stopped moving then. I'd felt her hand holding onto my arm, but her grip gradually fell away.

'NO!' I shouted. 'NO!'

Holding her tightly now, I began to cry, uncontrollably. This couldn't be real, could it? After a few seconds, I looked up at the faces of the people around me. They stood silently. Nobody spoke. It was like a bad dream, an absolute nightmare. But, it was real.

Then, still holding her tightly in my arms for a few moments, I saw two paramedics turn up, standing next to me.

'It's okay, fella. We're here to help you,' said the first paramedic, as he bent down next to me. I continued to hold Laura closely. He wanted to take her out of my arms. I glanced at him for a moment, with him beckoning his arms out towards us.

'It's okay. We want to help. Please, let us help,' he said.

I stared at him, moving my head to look at his female colleague. I didn't want to let Laura out of my grasp. I held Laura for a few seconds more until the female paramedic leant over us, touched my shoulder with her hand, and said, 'Please, let us help.'

I could hear pleading in her voice. I relaxed my grip on Laura as the paramedic helped me to my feet. Her colleague on the ground tried to find a pulse and began CPR, attempting to bring Laura back to life. Laura lay there motionless on that cold platform floor. The small crowd dispersed, drifting away in silence.

They tried to revive her for twenty minutes and finally looked at me as I stood over Laura. The paramedic guy stared at me and began moving his head from side to side, telling me visually that no, they couldn't revive her. 'I'm so sorry,' he said.

The station master had already brought out a canvas sheet that covered us from view of the remainder of the platform. The train had long departed whilst this all went on. Police had arrived at the scene shortly after the paramedics, which seemed unreal. I still thought it wasn't happening, even now. But it had.

It was supposed to be one of the happiest days of our lives. It had been. But not now. This day had been flipped on its head, instead becoming the worst day imaginable. It was tragic. Unbelievable.

Within an hour of agreeing to be my wife, she had become a heroine, saving a small boy's life. And she had paid the ultimate price. I was distraught. I sat on a bench at the station alone, shocked and stunned, a mere few feet away from Laura's body.

She was dead.

That was four days ago.

4. Mother's secret.

There was a knock at the door. I came back to now and to reality, still sitting in our flat above the shop, a mere four days after she'd gone. Dempsey had closed his shop in Hastings to run ours, as we were much busier than he was. And he wanted to be nearby. He'd lost his daughter. I'd been in our shop, but had had no heart for working there over the last few days since the accident, so Dempsey had taken over.

Getting out of my chair, I wandered to the front door of our flat. I could see the silhouette, in the glass panel, of a woman. As I opened the door, my mother walked straight past me, smiling like she always did. I did not smile back. It'd been four awful days since Laura had gone, and I'd not seen Mum since that day.

Turning towards me as she reached the living room and the settee I'd been sitting on, she said, 'Put that kettle on, Jack. We've got some talking to do.'

'Talk about what, Mum? I know you want to help, but Laura's dead,' I said, with my voice trailing off quietly, I'd not even wanted to say the last word.

'I'll put the kettle on then, son. Now go on. Go on. Sit there in the living room. I'm going to make you one of my sweet herbal teas. Go on, go and sit down. Listen to your mother now.' She smiled again. Sometimes, I couldn't figure her out.

On the day Laura had died, Mum had told me that she could help to bring her back. I thought she was absolutely crazy. We'd not spoken since then, as I'd ranted and raved at her, calling her all manner of names.

I sat down, looking out of the window towards the sea in the distance. After a few minutes of silence, she came in with our tea and gave me mine to drink. She sat down opposite me, in the old armchair she'd given us from her cottage. Mum knew it was my favourite chair, so she'd given it to us when we moved into the flat.

'Jack. Son. I do know how you feel.'

'How can you, Mum?'

'Remember your father died when you were younger. He was the love of my life, but I know we had more time together than you and Laura have had so far.'

'I know. I know. But this is so wrong, Mum. It's been four days. I don't want to eat. I don't want to sleep. I've been out each night walking on the beach on my own. I can't stop thinking of her. She lost her life saving a boy, little Tommy Jacobs. You know what a wonderful day it should've been, we'd planned to get married, she'd organised it all. I feel so lost.' I could feel the tears welling up in my eyes again, as I said this to her.

'Yes, I know. Is Harry here? He's been staying at my cottage since he came back yesterday. He went out earlier this morning with me, to go and see Laura at the parlour.'

'No. He called and said he'd be here later today, had to go to the library to check something out.'

'Oh. Well, I know you've been talking to him, and I'm glad. It'll help you, Jack.'

'Mum. There's nothing that can help me now, nothing at all.'

'Well, in this world, there're things we don't all understand. That's why I've come to talk to you again.'

'Understand what? That you live and you die?' I said, with anger in my voice. 'I know that your life can be ruined in an hour or less. And you telling me on the day she died that you can help. Are you nuts? How, Mum? What's the point to it all?' I shouted at her.

'Now then. I know you're heartbroken. Laura was always the only girl for you. From the day you two met, we all could see that you were meant to be together forever—as long as forever can last, as soul mates.'

'Mum. It's not fair. It just isn't. She was too young.' I whispered, now holding my head in my hands, looking down at the floor, not wanting to break down in floods of tears again.

There was a long silence then, and Mum wasn't smiling for once. We both sipped our tea. It was actually nice. I'd not tried her herbal tea since we were kids, when I was about fifteen, and I didn't like the taste then. But this sweet one she'd made was good.

'Listen, Jack,' she said, staring directly into my eyes as I raised my head . 'I'm going to tell you something that you won't believe. But just try and take it in. Just try. You know I said I can help a few days ago.'

'Huh. Nobody can help now. Nothing can bring her back.' I broke eye contact, to sip my tea.

'Please, son. Just hear me out.'

She stared at me again, and smiled once more, saying nothing for a few moments. I didn't speak either.

'My own mother was a seventh daughter. And you also know that I am a seventh daughter. Also, our Irish ancestry and heritage goes back centuries.'

'And what are you trying to say, Mum?'

'Well, there are factors here that could change your life.'

'What are you talking about?'

'You don't know that Dempsey is also a seventh son of a seventh son. He and I have known this since the first time he told me, many years ago when he visited, after his own wife had passed away. And he mentioned this when he and Laura visited our cottage that evening on your sixteenth birthday, all those years ago.'

'And?'

'And indeed, Jack. Throughout our history, it has been written in a Book of Scrolls that a gift can be bestowed upon the descendants of what we are, the seventh son and daughter of a seventh son and daughter.'

'Mum, you're not really making any sense to me here?'

'Just try and think about what I'm going to say now.'

She paused, and we silently sat for a few moments, sipping our tea again, until she took a deep breath and continued. 'What I've just said is important, Jack. You know that I've worked as a cleaner for many years. As well as this, you know I've read palms for many years. That is not a coincidence. It has been a calling. These last four days since Laura's accident, I've visited her and prayed for her. I've used certain incantations, which can help her on her journey. And I've convinced Dempsey that we can make it happen.'

'Make what happen, Mum?'

'The things I've told you are sacred, Jack. There is a way to help. There is a way to bring Laura back.'

I sat, open-mouthed, staring at her. Then I began to laugh. 'Mum! Are you still off your rocker? What the hell are you going on about? It's not possible for Laura to return. Don't you understand? She's DEAD!'

She moved from her chair and knelt right in front of me as I sat on the settee, and she held my hands in hers, as if we were both praying.

'I knew what your reaction would be, son. But please try and think. And listen to what I am saying to you. I know this sounds incredible, but we are in the eye of the storm right now. Time is an important factor. Please, please believe me. I know of a way to bring Laura back to you.'

I stared into Mum's eyes. She was right in front of me, still kneeling on the floor holding my hands tightly. By now, I'd stopped laughing.

'But how, Mum? This is not possible, nobody can make this happen. She's lying in the funeral parlour right now.'

'That's why I've visited her there, each of the last four days. I knew what your reaction would be, Jack. I've prayed over her body each day, but I can only do this within the seven days of her passing.'

'This is ridiculous! You're serious!'

Tears had formed in my eyes once again. I could feel them now running down my cheeks. As they did, Mum let go of my hands and rose to her feet, standing in front of me.

'Time's running out, son. There're only seven days for her return, and four days have almost gone after today, so we've only three left. Believe me when I say I've seen this in the Book of Scrolls. I cannot completely understand all of it, but it's possible only with a soul mate. You and Laura are just that. My readings over the years, with my stones, have allowed me to see things you could not understand, and I truly want to help you both.'

Staring at her as I stood up off the settee, I said, 'Go, Mum. Just go. This is ludicrous. How can you even think this?'

'Jack, I'm sorry, but this is your chance, a gift of life for Laura. You've not had the time together yet, that you should've had. The time is now to try and do something about it. Believe me, it can happen. It won't be easy, and you'll have to make big, big changes. But you've got to believe it can happen.'

'You're nuts, Mum!'

She smiled at me as I shouted those words at her. Then she got her coat, put it on, and said quietly in her soft Irish voice, 'Talk to your brother, Harry. Please, Jack. It's one chance. Please, talk to Harry.'

Kissing me on my cheek and hugging me, she turned away towards the front door, letting herself out of our flat, leaving me standing there alone again.

Talking out loud to myself after she'd left I said, 'What the hell was that all about? My mum's lost the plot, surely? Or has she? This is just so, so, unbelievable. Bloody crazy!'

I finished my herbal tea, thinking more about what Mum had said, still talking to myself. 'She used to read palms as well as tea leaves, and used her stones to give people readings about their lives. I remember her doing that when I was younger. And she was always talking about our Irish ancestry, and I already knew she was a seventh daughter. But I didn't know my grandmother was a seventh daughter as well. Nor did I know about Dempsey, either.'

Was there a chance? She'd said speak to Harry. What could he know? He'd been in Ireland for his priesthood, but could he help? This all seemed too incredible to comprehend.

As I walked around the flat, I pondered this for about an hour after Mum had left. Then, even though I knew he was coming round, I finally decided that I had to call Harry. My mind was racing as I started to think that there might really be a chance. Maybe, just maybe, anything could happen.

Picking up my mobile phone, I decided to call Harry...

5. Harry's advice.

I dialled the number to Harry's mobile, and he answered it immediately.

'How you doing, Jack?'

'Okay, Harry. You fancy popping around for a chat? I've had a visit from Mum.'

'Yep, of course. I was on my way, but give me half an hour and I'll be with you. Get the kettle on shortly, bro.'

'Will do. See you in a while.'

It was about twenty minutes before Harry arrived. I'd only seen him for about ten minutes since he'd arrived and he'd mentioned nothing about what Mum had said. I looked out of the window towards the sea again on this still, murky, dull, January day; just four days after losing Laura. There was a knock at the door. I walked through the flat knowing—and hoping now—that it would be Harry.

'Well, are you gonna let me in or not, Jack?' questioned my brother Harry, standing at the front door. Even though I'd only seen him briefly yesterday, with him being aware of Laura's demise, it was good to have him back, but for how long, who knew?

'Er, yep. Yep, of course, Harry,' I said, in a daze, with my mind still wandering to the memory of how Laura and I had first met, and what Mum had been saying only about an hour or so earlier.

Harry was not as tall as me, and unlike my own dark brown hair, he had fine, blond, straight hair. He was more muscular than me, which he constantly used to remind me of when we were younger. But the one thing Harry had was maturity beyond his twenty-four years, and he was extremely wise. In school and at university he'd been top of the class, especially in his chosen field, astrology and astrophysics. But he'd always wanted to be a priest, as he'd been fascinated by religion, the church, and the possibility of the afterlife.

As he walked into our flat, he stared at me intensely, before saying questioningly, 'Well?' Then he hugged me tightly, and I hugged him in return.

I replied, 'Come into the living room. And what does "well" mean, then?' I turned away to lead the way into the room.

'You know damn well, Jack! It's been four days since you've spoken to Mum. That's too long, and you know it!' he said, in an angry and emotional voice. That wasn't like Harry, I thought. He was always calm. Continuing, he said more calmly, 'I don't know what happened the day Laura passed away, between you and Mum. She won't tell me, but I know that something's wrong, and I know she can help.'

'So you know something's wrong, do you?' I replied, turning to stare into his face. 'And what good would it do talking to her at all, Harry? She's got a bloody screw loose! She's been here earlier today, and told me again she can bring Laura back. It's madness! It's not possible, is it?' I questioned my own doubts and thought that maybe—just maybe—it could happen. 'It hurts like hell!' I shouted at him. 'How can I live without her? I don't want to.'

There was silence between us then, with neither of us speaking for what seemed like hours, but was in fact a long couple of minutes as we both sat next to each other on the settee.

'Hey, listen to me,' said Harry finally, in a softer voice than before. 'You have a wonderful family around you. We're all here for you.'

'She's gone, and I want her back. None of this seems real.'

Standing up, I stared at my brother, knowing I could always talk to him. He understood me so well, it was as if he had a sixth sense about me, and I did about him. I continued to tell him about Mum's visit.

'Okay, Harry. Mum came round about an hour ago, and said again that she knows a way to bring Laura back. I told her she's crazy and she told me to speak to you. You know I trust you with my life and always will. After speaking to her, I thought about what she said, and she sewed a seed in my mind that this could maybe—as ridiculous as it sounds—just maybe, work. Look, on the day Laura died, Mum said she could help to bring her back. I told her then she was mad and I didn't speak to her until today. She told me I had to speak to you. She said that there's seven days to bring Laura back and four have gone by already. What do you think, Harry? Is this for real?'

We'd made our way into the kitchen, with Harry leading the way. I stopped to switch the kettle on. I knew he loved his tea. He never drank alcohol, being in the priesthood it was forbidden, though he had no interest in it anyway.

Harry sat down on the chair in the kitchen, waiting for the kettle to boil, and there was silence between us again. I began crying to myself, but Harry could see me and got back out of his chair and cuddled me as I began to sob uncontrollably. It was good to have him back for a while, even in these circumstances.

After a few moments, the kettle boiled. Harry let his vice-like grip ease, returning to his chair. Neither of us said a word as I made the tea.

'Okay then,' he said. 'I believe her, Jack. If you think about it, there's always been strange things happening around us. You know it, if you really think about it, don't you?' he said, with pleading in his voice.

I replied, my voice croaking with emotion and tears rolling down my cheeks, 'So, maybe I do. But what am I supposed to do now? Crikey, I'd not spoken to her for four days until earlier. That's unforgivable in my book. I know our Mum's a wonderful woman, but will she really give this a go? It seems incredible to believe that what she said can happen. I'm not sure about this at all.

'But hey,' I continued, with excitement in my voice now, 'I remember now what grandma used to say when we were small boys, that she believed it was possible to return to life. Maybe—what d' you think Harry—can it really happen?'

'Right, then. I believe the answer is yes.' Harry said. 'You know what you've got to do.'

'What?' I replied, with a dizzy head now, thoughts all merging into confusion in my head.

'Come on, Jack, all you've got to do is pick up the phone. Call her. You told me just now that Mum said there's not much time. So call her. I believe it can happen. Call her now!' he pleaded with me.

'What, right now?' I said.

'Yes, now!' he replied. 'You've hardly spoken to her. There's only seven days to do this, with four wasted already. She wants to help, and we've always known she's got strange ways about her, so call her now, you idiot! She can help, and so can I!' He was shouting at me, with tears in his eyes. 'But before you call her, Jack, listen to me. Right now.'

'What is it?' I looked at him quizzically before he continued.

'Mum asked you to talk to me for a reason.'

'Go on then, what is it?'

There was a pause and a long silence before he spoke again, taking a sip of tea. 'Well, I've been studying a lot in the seminary, as you probably know. What Mum says has an element of truth to it. In my readings, I found the Book of Scrolls mentioned many times, although it cannot all be read in English. The original book is actually in my seminary, in County Tyrone! Much of it is written in an ancient Gaelic language, not used or known widely now. I've learnt much of this language myself, through the elderly priesthood, and there is a way for this to happen, like I said. Firstly, you have to believe and have faith in what you want to do, Jack. Secondly, you are soul mates with Laura. Thirdly, it can only be achieved by the seventh son and daughter of a seventh son and daughter. That is Mum and Laura's father. And fourthly, Mum also has the ancient stones, and we both know that she used to use incantations with them in her palm readings, when we used to live as boys in the cottage. Besides this, she's been praying with her stones and incantations every day for an hour at Laura's side, since she passed away, at the funeral parlour. These one hour prayers are keeping Laura with us, because there really is only seven days to make this happen.'

'So, you believe this, Harry?'

'Yes, I do. I truly believe. But there is some ancient text that I cannot translate in that book, Jack. It's to do with night and day, plus darkness and light. I've not managed to understand it yet, but I've been to the library here to check out if there was some other information that could help—but we're running out of time. I was at the library when you called me.'

I stared at Harry, open mouthed. It was real. It could happen. He looked at me and pointed to my mobile phone and nodded at me. He didn't have to tell me what to do, as I called Mum there and then. I was agog, with what he'd said.

Calling her number, I was aware that she didn't have, on her landline phone, the facility to know who was calling her. Harry had set up her phone on a visit a couple of years ago, because he was brilliant with all things technological, and he'd told me then that Mum didn't need to know who would be calling. She'd told him back then she'd know anyway.

That was another strange quirk about her, because she did always know if any of us called her.

I held the phone to my ear. Harry was waiting and watching me, and I heard the ringing tone four times.

Then she answered the phone.

Instantly she said, 'Hello, Jack. I've been waiting for you to call. I take it Harry is with you right now. You don't have to know how I know, as he hasn't told me. Check with him after we've spoken. I know you don't quite believe completely what's going on, but like I said four days ago, and earlier today, I can help. So, jump in your car and come to the cottage as quickly as you can. Time is running out and I'll see you soon and explain, son. Drive safely. I love you. Your brother knows a great deal more to help us, so tell him I love him too. Goodbye,' she said and the phone line went dead.

I looked at my mobile phone in my hand with an open mouth again, and in disbelief.

Then I looked at Harry, who was staring at me. 'Well, what did she say?' he said.

'Well, I...' I started to say to him, but I couldn't speak. I didn't know what to say.

Looking back at the phone in my hand, I heard the buzzing noise of a call that had ended, and it sparked my mind back to life.

Harry walked over to me, took the phone out of my hand and said, 'Hey, is everything okay? You never said a word to Mum. Are you alright?'

'Well,' I finally said, after gathering my thoughts for a few seconds. 'She knew it was me. How does she do that, Harry? She always knows when it's us.' I stared at him before continuing, 'She said to go over to the cottage, so I'm going. Right now. Mum said there's not much time. She said she loved us both. You know what, Harry, I believe her. And you. I really believe it!'

He stared at me and just said, 'Go. Go!' He was still holding my mobile phone in his hand.

I raced from the kitchen towards the front door grabbing my car keys on the way. I turned at the doorway with Harry looking on as he said, 'Believe, Jack. Believe, brother. This can happen, for you and Laura.'

Staring back at him, I nodded to say yes, and he handed my phone back to me. Then, we hugged each other again. Looking at his face, I could see he still had tears in his eyes. I said, 'Thanks, Harry. You're the best.' I kissed him on his cheek, then turned to go to our car to drive to Mum's.

But as we released our embrace, he grabbed my arm turning me back towards him, and said, 'It'll all work out, Jack. Listen to her. She's never let us down. I've got to go back to the library before it closes. We'll speak later.'

I tried to smile, but the tears wouldn't let me. Harry said, 'Go on. Get out of here. Go!'

Managing to get my thoughts back, I said, 'Okay. Thanks for the advice.'

Then I turned towards the front door, leaving Harry in our flat, closing the door behind me. Going down the stairs and getting to the car, wiping the tears from my face and eyes, I began to have hope. Just a small glimmer of hope, thinking to myself that this could really happen.

So, I left to drive to Mum's, not knowing what to expect, but hoping. Really, truly hoping, saying to myself, 'Believe this, Jack Stanton. Believe it. You know they're right. We can do this... '

6. The mysterious gift.

Driving in the car—our old reliable BMW—towards Mum's cottage, I realised it was day four of seven. Time really was running out now. When I'd driven the couple of miles and parked outside, she was waiting at the front door to let me in.

'Come on, the drinks are ready. Straight into the kitchen with you,' she said, as she ushered me inside the cottage.

Another one of her herbal teas awaited me; she must've known I'd liked the one she'd made earlier in the day at our place, as I couldn't remember if I'd told her or not. I sat down in the kitchen, having said nothing.

'Okay. Firstly, I've cancelled the registry office for your wedding as it was only going to be a small affair. Now I'm going to explain to you what's going to happen. You won't remember it all, but your brother is aware of it, more than you'll ever know. He wanted me to explain it all to you. And Dempsey knows too.'

'So, er, Harry said you'd been to pray each day with Laura?'

'Yes, and I have to until the seventh day, Jack. Now, just listen,' she said in her Irish voice, being more authoritative than ever. She put her finger to her mouth, and I saw she meant me to be quiet. I listened.

'We only have seven days because of the fact that Dempsey and myself are seventh born of seventh born.

For this to work, that has to be true and it is. You also have to believe, Jack. I know now that you do. You wouldn't be here m'boy, unless you did. I have the stones, prayers, and incantations. And The Book of Scrolls describes where and when it can take place. Harry is working on that at the library right now. He knows when, but not exactly where, though he has an idea, although he's not fully translated everything yet. He'll let us know later today, once he's finished at the library.'

'This is unbelievable, but I believe it, Mum!'

'Good. And the most important point is that we have the seven days as well, though you know we've wasted four already. This is a gift, Jack. That's how long it took to create life by our Lord. It's all real, son. I've known this was a possibility since my own mother told me the story when I was fourteen years old, about the seventh born son and daughter, passing down the possibility of a gift to their own seventh born son and daughter. I never expected to be in a position to try, but I believe its right to do so.' She paused to have a sip of her tea. I just carried on staring at her.

I was about to speak when she put her hand up in front of my face to stop me from speaking, and then put her finger to her mouth again, meaning for me to be silent. Then she continued.

'Now—like I've said—we've had four days almost past, of the seven allowed. There is much to do, Jack. Your shop will continue to be run by Dempsey. He is distraught by the loss of his daughter, but he wants to help. He's unsure whether this is right or not, but he'll help us. Harry's working on the exact location we need to go to. The incantations I know from my own experience. The stones I have, bar one. The location of this one stone Harry's working on as well. That's why Dempsey's concerned, as he feels Laura won't be able to return fully without all four of them. You will not know, but my stones are all from one particular piece, which was broken into four fragments, of which I have three. Believe me when I say that I know this will work, because your brother thinks and hopes he has found the location of the fourth fragment, if we need it. There is a price to pay, but that is of no consequence right now, I can explain that to you later. Things can change in the flicker of a heartbeat, Jack, and I believe this was sent to try our faith and test us all.'

There was silence for a few moments before I spoke. 'Mum, this all sounds like fantasy—but its reality. I know that now, I really do.'

My head was spinning. But it was happening.

'Your brother will be back from the library soon, and he'll hopefully have the information we need for the location of the fourth stone and where we have to take Laura, if we need to. He's the only one who understands the language almost completely, Jack. Now, you've to go home, lock up the flat, and call Dempsey. Tell him that you know everything now and we need his help. Today's the fourth day, and it's almost evening now, so we've only the three days left. He's unsure, Jack, he's concerned about darkness and light for Laura. You've got to convince him that this is for the best. It's a once in a lifetime chance that'll never come again. This really is a gift for you to get her back. Prove to Dempsey we need him. Go Jack, time's-a-wasting.'

I got out of my chair, having finished my tea, and Mum rose from hers at the same time. We hugged, saying nothing. It was all about time now, and we didn't have much left to make it work. This was actually happening. It was real. And I now had to talk to Dempsey to ensure he would help.

7. Dempsey

Leaving Mum's, I knew I had to convince Dempsey that this was the right thing to do. He was a good man, with a soft Irish voice himself, having inherited the antique business from his own parents. He'd lost Laura's mother when she was young, so he may be sympathetic, I thought. I went to the shop to check it was already closed and locked the flat up before driving to his house on the outskirts of town. I decided not to call, but to just turn up. I knew he had had a reputation as a drinker and womaniser in his distant past, before I'd known him, but now he was in his fifties and more settled, so he should be home by now, I hoped.

Arriving at his home on this cold January evening, I got out of the car and knocked on his front door.

'Hello, Jack,' he said, opening the door, slurring. I could smell he'd been drinking. For many years since I'd first known him, he'd not been drinking heavily, until Laura and I moved in above the shop a few years ago. But this evening, he looked three parts to the wind—alcohol induced.

'Hey Dempsey, want to go inside? Be nice to have a chat.'

'Yep, sure Jack. You fancy a drink, fella? One for Laura?'

'Let's get inside first, shall we?' Then I helped him into the house, going to the kitchen. I put the kettle on, noticing a half empty bottle of whisky as I did, next to the bread bin.

'You know what, I could've never wished for a better son-in-law than you. What happened, Jack? Where's Laura?'

He was drunk. There was no point talking to him much, in the state he was in right now. I managed to get him from the kitchen into the living room, where I sat him down on a comfy chair.

'You sit there, Dempsey, and relax. We'll have a chat in a while.'

Within minutes he'd fallen asleep. I waited, watching him and listening to him talking gibberish whilst he slept. I'd not seen him like this for a long time. But it was understandable. He'd lost his daughter. For some reason the last thing I wanted to do was drink alcohol. I made myself a cup of tea and listened to the radio quietly while I waited. I couldn't believe it when our song, 'Our Day Will Come', came on. It was an old one that we used to sing to each other, not long after we'd first met. It was beautiful, we'd both thought. Laura had it on a CD and introduced me to other songs by the artist. I welled up again, turning the radio off when the song finished. I was so tired, I started to fall asleep myself, my mind swimming with memories of Laura.

After about an hour, I woke, and Dempsey began to stir and wake himself.

When he came to, he said, 'What're you doing here, Jack?'

'Came to see you, Dempsey. You feeling better now? I'll make you a coffee.'

'That'd be nice. Thanks.'

I went to the kitchen and left him to come round for a while, returning a few minutes later with a black coffee for him and a cup of tea for myself.

'I think I need a quick wash, Jack. I won't be a minute,' Dempsey said, getting out of his chair, then going upstairs to the bathroom. I heard the splosh and splash of water from the sink, where he must've washed his face off to try and sober up, then I heard the thud of his footsteps returning back downstairs.

When he returned, he walked straight into the living room where he'd fallen asleep, looking more refreshed.

'Okay, get that coffee down you, it'll help, I hope.'

'Ah! Thanks, Jack. You're a good 'un, you are.'

'That's as maybe. Right, I'll get straight to the point. I've been told of what you know about already, Dempsey. Mum's explained to me about you and her being the seventh born of the seventh born, and the implications for Laura. You know there's a way of bringing her back, don't you?'

'I do. But it's dangerous. I don't know if it's the right thing to do or not. Your mum's convinced of it. And Harry's working on the where and when, as well. I'm worried, Jack, what will happen if it doesn't work properly?'

'What do you mean?'

'Well, if it goes wrong, she could be roaming around earth as a spirit. That would be awful, Jack. Do you want that on your conscience if it goes wrong? Remember, I told you to look after her years ago. If this is a disaster,

I'll still hold you responsible. Maybe she should be left to rest.'

'You shouldn't think like that, Dempsey.'

'But someone's got to, Jack! If it goes wrong, whose fault is it? It'll be yours, because you want this. She died. Is this morally right in the eyes of our Lord?'

'Don't you want your daughter back?'

'Listen. I know how it can happen, I've spoken to your mother earlier today. She told me, before you arrived at her cottage, said she'd be telling you everything she knows. Fine woman, Mary.'

'And what's the problem?'

There was a silence then, before he spoke again.

'What's the problem? Well, this is a resurrection, that's exactly what it is! It's not supposed to be humanly possible at all. But you and I, Harry, and your mother know from our history and The Book of Scrolls that it is possible. What I'm saying, Jack, is it's ONLY POSSIBLE. There is no one hundred percent guarantee that she'll come back. I don't want my daughter roaming the plains of this earth in a kind of limbo land, or something like that. It's morally wrong. I know Mary's been praying each of these last four days, to keep Laura with us in the funeral parlour, along with her stones. We're creating the possibility of a good against evil scenario here. I'm saying that this is something we can't control. And it's worrying the hell out of me! As far as I know, this has never, ever happened before. Nobody knows if it'll work, or where she'll end up. Does anyone want the responsibility of this, Jack? I know I don't. She may be better off dead. I don't know. I just don't know where this'll lead, and the implications it's going to have on all of us. It could open up a gateway to hell. Who knows?'

'Look. I've only heard stories about the Book of Scrolls until today, but I know Mum and Harry have knowledge of what's inside, especially Harry. You know I want her back. I'm supposed to be with her. Why, only four days ago, we decided to get married. You know that. I don't care about morals and good against evil. Until a few hours ago, I'd been grieving for her. Now I've got a chance to have her back. I believe it, Dempsey. I truly believe this. It's one God damned chance I'm prepared to take, and I need your help. Please, if I have to beg you, I will!' I said, with tears in my eyes. 'How can you be against it? She's your daughter!'

'Right. Listen to me again, Jack. You know you're like a son to me. Always have been, since you and Laura started out together years ago. If I'd had a son, then I'd have wanted him to be like you. I can speak no higher of you than that. But this is bereavement you are going through right now. I'll say again, in the eyes of our Lord, there was only ever one resurrection. This would be seen by many as against God's holy law. But, because of all of our knowledge, and because it's my daughter, I will do this, for you. Only for you and Laura, Jack. But mark my words, if this doesn't work, I'll hold you personally responsible if she fails to return! Remember that, Jack. I promise I will hunt you down, wherever you may go, if my daughter is left between heaven and earth. I promise you!'

I stared at Dempsey for a few seconds. His eyes looked wild, as if still intoxicated from the alcohol he'd consumed until I'd arrived to sober him up. But they were not drunken eyes, they were crazy with anger.

'I'll make sure it works, Dempsey. Believe me. You know I love Laura. I'd do anything to have her back. It'll work. It'll work.'

There was a silence, and I saw the pulsing veins in his forehead recede. I thought to myself then that it had to work. I was relying on my mother and brother to help with details I knew little about. But I had to trust them. It would be okay, it would work out. It had to. We didn't have much time left now.

'Just tell me where I need to be and when, Jack. I don't agree with this, but I won't let you down m'boy,' Dempsey said, solemnly.

'It's day four of seven now, so I'll get back to you as soon as I know where we have to be. But do one thing for me.'

'What's that?'

'No more drinking Dempsey, not until this is over. Please?'

'All right. Okay. You know this was a sort of one off, don't you?'

'Yep, I do. You're a good man. You've been a good dad, and you've been to hell and back yourself. I'll be in touch,' I said, and I walked out of the living room, wiping the tears from my eyes, going towards the front door.

As I opened the door, he called out to me. 'Hey Jack, just a minute.'

Turning back from the front door, I could see him bounding down the hallway towards me. He reached out to hug me and said. 'I'm sorry, I don't want to be a killjoy, just practical. I know what loss is like. But a part of me has a mass of anger about all of this. I love you and Laura. Heed my words though. Now get gone to your mother's.'

I left his house. The experience of speaking to Dempsey was tough. I hadn't thought he'd object to this at all. His own strong Irish religious beliefs must have gone against what we were trying to do. This went against anything I'd ever known myself. Now, I'd sort of got him on our side. Getting into the car, I drove back to Mum's to discuss where to go next and what to do. Harry was getting information from the library.

I didn't know where it'd happen, or exactly when, other than it would be within the next three days. And time was running out, fast...

8. Plan of action.

As I arrived back at Mum's cottage from Dempsey's house, it was late in the evening on day four. Harry hadn't yet returned from the library. There had been no call from him on his mobile, either, and he didn't reply when I tried contacting him.

'How'd it go with Dempsey?' questioned Mum, as I went to open her front door. She was already at the door, opening it, as I leant forward to put my key in the door to open it.

'Well, he's agreed to help us still.' I said as she held the door open for me.

'Good. We need him,' she said, not smiling as usual.

'But he's not happy about it. Anything goes wrong and it's all my fault. He's concerned that this could open up some sort of conflict between good and evil.'

'Well, he's got a point.'

I followed her into the kitchen. She'd already made us both a cup of tea, ready and hot for drinking. We sat at the table and she continued.

'Did he tell you that this is a form of resurrection?'

'Yes he did.'

'And what do you think about it? Do you think it's good against evil and we are playing with powers that we shouldn't be involved with? Do you think that it's morally right or wrong to try and bring her back?'

'Well, we haven't got all of the information from Harry yet, but I know that I love her, Mum. I want her back. I think this can work. I believe, and that's enough for me. I'll try anything, now I understand what you and Harry know.'

'Good. You've got the faith Jack, just like your brother.'

'Thanks.'

Sipping her tea, she smiled, then nodded at me. 'It'll be tough. We've not a lot of time. So listen. When Harry returns, with luck he'll have all of the details we need. That's if he's managed to obtain the information about the Book of Scrolls more fully at the library. He may be able to tell us where we need to go. I know we need the stones, incantations and all of us. But Harry knows—I hope—the rest.'

'Okay, so where is he?'

'Still not back from the library yet, it must've shut a couple of hours ago. He should've been here by now, I've been waiting for him since you went to go and see Dempsey. I've tried to call him on his mobile phone, but he's not answered.'

'I know, I've left a message for him and he's not called me back either. We've not got much time, so tell me what else to do.'

'Well, you know I've been praying at Laura's side at the funeral parlour, with my stones. What you've got to do, is find a way of getting her out of there without anyone being suspicious. Normally the body—Laura—is left until the burial. She's still in the same clothing as the day she passed over. You know, it was her internal organs that were crushed and damaged, which stopped her breathing. I'm sorry to bring this up Jack, but I know you know this already. With her return, there are things that may change for her, though she'll return to full normal health with a price to pay. I'll explain that to you when she's back with us.'

'Mum, you mentioned this "price to pay" before. What d'you mean?'

'Nothing to worry about son, I just mean that we can only try and make this happen just the once. There's no other price to pay other than anything your brother may find. It'll be fine, believe me. You have faith now, and believe, so with that faith, anything can truly happen.'

'Okay then. As long as there's nothing else.'

'Not that concerns you.'

As she spoke, my mobile phone went off, and I didn't question her further. It was Harry.

'Hey Harry, where've you been?'

'I'm on my way to you now. Had my phone on silent in the library, didn't see your missed call until a moment ago. Mum with you?'

'Yep, she's here. And I've been to see Dempsey as well.'

'What did he say? You know we need him.'

'He'll help.'

'Right. Good. I'll be with you and Mum in ten minutes. I'll explain everything else to you when I arrive.'

'Okay. Drive safe, Harry, see you shortly.'

He cut off his phone. I knew he'd been using Mum's old car since he'd come back from Ireland.

'Harry's about ten minutes away, Mum. He's on his way.'

'Good. I'll put the kettle on for him now, and we'll wait. You put the radio on for a while.'

Which is exactly what I did. I put the radio on for a bit of background music to try and keep some sanity in my own mind. I couldn't believe the song that came straight on again. Ironically, it was our song, 'Our Day Will Come'. I sat in the chair and began to cry quietly all to myself. Had Mum known that'd be on the radio? Or was it just a weird coincidence? I sat and listened to the song, wiping tears from my eyes as I did. When it had finished, Mum came in with Harry's tea and sat next to me on her settee. Within seconds of her sitting down, there was a knock at the door, so I got up, turned the radio off, and opened the door to greet Harry. He didn't have a key anymore, since moving to Ireland.

Harry walked into the cottage behind me, taking off his coat and putting the car keys on the table. Then he sat down and picked up his tea, sipping it before speaking. 'So, you know some of the plan, Jack? I'm not going to mince my words. Maybe there's not enough time. But we've got to try. Mum, have you asked him about getting Laura out of the funeral parlour?'

'Yes son, he knows to get her out, but neither of us know where we need to go.'

'Okay then. I've been a long time, as I had to read through some information at the library regarding sacred grounds in the area. There is only one place that's possible for us to use here.'

'Well, where is it, Harry?' I said, as he'd stopped talking to sip his tea again.

'A shrine is needed. The only one near, with the timescale we have, is at St. Augustine's. The chapel there has an ancient shrine. We need that. Plus, the stones, Mum's incantations and Dempsey. That's why I've been so long, I had to go to the chapel after visiting the library.'

'That's good, son. Now, Jack, we've got to get Laura there by the seventh day. It's the one chance to make this work. That's Sunday. Have you thought of a way to get her there yet?'

'Not really, Mum. You got any ideas, or you Harry?'

'Well, I think I've got a plan. What with me being a priest and all. I've visited her on my own, so we need to go together. I can speak to the funeral directors and ask for Laura to be brought back to either Dempsey's, or here to Mum's cottage.'

'With Dempsey's frame of mind, it'd be better for her to come here,' I said.

'Right o' then. Sounds good. What do you think Mum?' replied Harry.

'It makes sense. You know it does. So do you, Jack. We've to get her to St. Augustine's chapel and the shrine, so suspicion will not be on us, with you being a priest temporarily in residence here. But how will we transport her to here?'

We all stopped talking for a moment until Harry continued.

'Everyone who may have a suspicion will simply think that she's been moved because of the emotional turmoil we're all in. That's fine and won't be a problem.

The real issue to overcome will be getting her, from here to the chapel and shrine.'

We sat silently again, knowing that we had to resolve this. How could we move her without people questioning why?

Then I had the moment when the light bulb goes on in your brain.

'I've got it!' I shouted.

'What?' asked Mum.

'Jack, it's got to be believable y'know?' said Harry.

'Well, it's pretty obvious, really. If we bring her back here we can explain to everyone that we want the funeral procession to leave from here in the next few days. We can arrange what day that'll be, hopefully Sunday, saying we're having a service at the chapel for her, with our own private burial after the service.'

'One problem with that, Jack. The chapel doesn't have funeral services on a Sunday. I wasn't there long, but I saw the resident priest briefly and explained our situation. He said it was rare for a funeral service to be held on a Sunday.'

'Thought about that one. You're a qualified priest now, almost. They have church services at the chapel on a Sunday morning. Surely you can arrange for us to be there for the service in the afternoon or evening?' I questioned.

'Well, the vicar said it was rare for a Sunday burial, but he didn't say no. I'll go back tomorrow morning first thing, and try and arrange our service for Sunday afternoon or early evening. That'll be the seventh day. What with me being a priest, I should be able to swing it, as long as they have no other events planned; that'd be unusual on a Sunday afternoon or evening anyway.'

'It'll work out, both of you,' said Mum. 'You've got the faith now, Jack. Harry's always had it. Now, seeing as it's a small chapel, let's see, tomorrow, when you go there Harry—along with Jack—what the priest says. Either way, we must get her there. It's the only place near enough for us to use.'

'That way then, Mum, if we have the service conducted by Harry, our family and friends who can make it will be there at St. Augustine's to say goodbye to her. But if this works, and she returns, what'll I say to everyone then?'

'Son, you'll have to make a big change. Close the shop. Sell up. Move away. You cannot live here with Laura anymore. Explain it to Dempsey. Everyone will know that she's departed. They would have seen it with their own eyes. Only we will know otherwise. You will need to arrange a fresh start. Harry, you know where possibly, don't you?'

'Yes Mum, I do. Jack, you know that the three stones are needed and the fourth one is missing. I know where it is and we don't think we'll need it. But if we do, we have our old Uncle Sidney—Mum's cousin—to thank for its existence and I know exactly where it is.'

'Where, Harry?'

'You may not like this, Jack, it's a long way away.'

'Doesn't matter. You say we may not need it. I hope not. But if we do, where is it?'

'In America.'

'America!' I shouted.

There was silence for a few moments before Mum spoke again.

'The original stones I have are from one tablet, as you know, broken into four pieces, of which I have three. My cousin Sidney knew of the Book of Scrolls, though it wasn't common knowledge. Many years ago, he convinced a wealthy American that the one stone he possessed had mystical powers, and he duly sold it, not actually realising its true potential. Neither did he realise its true value; he only wanted to make money from it. My cousin was a budding entrepreneur in his youth.'

'Jack, I know this sounds crazy. But listen,' said Harry. 'Mum's right. That's why I've been at the library. I've been checking the whereabouts of this fourth stone, if we need it, and who it was sold to by dear old silly Uncle Sid. That was before I went to the chapel. It's in America, Jack. And it's safe for now. In a museum.'

'So let's hope we don't need it, there's not much time left.'

'Jack, trust me. I know you do. We've got a plan now. Keep the faith and it'll all work out. Tomorrow, we'll go to the funeral parlour, arrange for Laura to come here, and we'll get the service arranged for Sunday afternoon as well, when we both visit the chapel to organise it. That doesn't leave much time, but it's enough. After the service, we can all stay at the chapel. I know where the shrine is now, after my visit today. If we need the other stone, I know where it is, like I said. And don't forget my reading of the Book of Scrolls gives me more knowledge than even Mum. Trust me, brother.'

'I believe you, Harry. But just in case, where in America is this stone? You said it's in a museum, but where?'

'New York, Jack. New York.'

'Well, I s'pose that's good. At least if it doesn't work out, there's a chance for Laura still,' I said.

'That's right, son. Trust in us. We all have faith. Now we've got a plan, it's time for another cuppa and I'll make us some dinner, as it's getting late. I think you'd both better sleep here tonight, and then get off early tomorrow morning. That'll be day five, and we've all got to keep focused on what we're doing. I'll put the kettle on, then,' Mum said, taking our cups, and going into the kitchen.

'Thanks, Mum,' Harry and I said in unison. Then we looked at each other and smiled. I loved my brother. He and Mum had given Laura a chance, against all worldly odds. Now I really believed we had a plan that could work. But I was concerned about Dempsey all the same. I had told Mum and Harry that he'd blame me for everything, but I hadn't told them he'd hunt me down if it went wrong. With all they were doing, I just couldn't tell them that. I hoped and prayed that all of the planning would work out.

9. Days five and six of seven.

The next two days went by in a blur.

After visiting Laura with Mum and Harry, we arranged for her to be returned to the cottage. I'd not visited the funeral parlour at all since the accident. I couldn't bring myself to go. Now, though, after seeing her, Mum had convinced me that she was in a deep sleep and not dead. I had believed her and whispered to Laura that we would be back together soon.

Paperwork had to be signed for Laura's release, but this allowed Mum to continue her prayers and incantations with the stones without fear of interruption once she was back with us at the cottage.

Dempsey was not happy, but understood what was happening.

Harry and I went to St. Augustine's chapel, on day five, to arrange the service. Fortunately, it went well, with Harry swinging it for our own personal service on the Sunday afternoon, conducting it himself as a private family affair. And once the service was over, we'd be taking Laura for a private and personal burial in the chapel grounds, all arranged by Harry.

We made phone calls on days five and six, speaking to family and friends to let them know that we were having a small service at the chapel, telling them that we had no plans for a get together afterwards. We were sorry for the short notice, but understood if some of them couldn't make it. Mum organised the hearse—

even at this short notice—as one of her old clients who worked at the funeral parlour, was happy to help us.

So far, the plan was working and on the morning of the service, we had several family and friends who came to the cottage to say farewell to Laura. It was a tough morning, but by mid-afternoon we were all ready to go to the chapel, knowing that what we had planned after the service was close at hand. All of our family and friends who visited over the last couple of days had said some wonderful things about Laura. They'd all left the cottage now, leaving us alone with her, as we waited to go to the chapel. It was day seven. We knew there wasn't a lot of time left now.

10. The seventh day.

Once we were all ready at the cottage, Mum, Harry, Dempsey and I gathered in the downstairs parlour room around Laura. It was time to take her into the back of the hearse, to be sealed for the first time.

Leaning over her, I whispered quietly so that nobody could hear me, 'Hey baby, not long now and we'll be reunited. I love you, Laura Dempsey. My turn to be on the ball with everything now.'

'You okay, Jack?' asked Harry as I was whispering.

'Yep, fine. And you?'

He nodded. 'Time to go shortly. Let's get this over with. It'll all work out, trust me. Once the service is over this afternoon, we'll thank everyone for coming and give them our apologies for the short notice again. They need never know why.'

Harry and I then sealed the lid over Laura in silence, for what we hoped would be just a short time only, for the journey to the chapel.

'You two boys all right?' said Dempsey.

'They're as good as can be expected under the circumstances. We've got a long day ahead of us, that'll likely change all of our lives forever, don't y'know,' said Mum, quietly and seriously.

We all four stood silently glancing at each other for a few moments before Harry spoke. 'Right, are we all set then?' We'd finished closing the coffin lid down. 'Time to go. I'll sit in the front seat of the hearse with you, Jack.

Mum, you and Dempsey are to go in the second car, along with Richard Leonard, as planned.'

'Where is Richard?' said Mum.

'He's outside waiting,' said Harry. 'Said he'd leave us alone to say our last goodbyes before we carry Laura out into the car. Jack, it's time I think. Er, Dempsey, can you call Richard back in please, we need him to help us carry the coffin now.'

'Will do.'

When Dempsey went outside, Harry continued to speak. 'Once we're at the chapel, and the service is over and everyone has gone, you know what we've to do. The shrine is outside the chapel, so we'll have to carry Laura out. Fortunately, it'll be dark this time of year. The shrine's at the back of the chapel, and there's no exterior door, so we'll have to walk through the entrance with her. Mum, you've got to make sure there's no one around. There shouldn't be by then, as I've explained to the vicar at St. Augustine's it'll only be us left there afterwards. Dempsey knows about this already, so it's all under control. No problems regarding the burial, either, that's been taken care of under my jurisdiction, as you know.'

When Richard returned with Dempsey, we proceeded to carry Laura from Mum's cottage, placing her into the hearse for our journey to the chapel. We did so, in complete silence.

Once she was safely in the vehicle, we got into the cars. It would take about half an hour to travel to the chapel. It was another cold day in early January. Harry was dressed in his full priest regalia, prepared for the service. Sitting in the car next to each other, we both sat in silence. We'd discussed everything already, several times, about how we were going to get Laura out of the chapel to the old external shrine, so everything was set.

After about twenty-five minutes, we arrived at the chapel and, getting out of the car, I broke the silence.

'There's got to be about three hundred people here, Harry. How're they all going to get into the chapel? I thought there'd only be about forty or fifty people here to pay their respects.'

'They all know about Laura's tragic accident, Jack. Don't worry about that now. Concentrate on what we've got to do. The local vicar is organising how to get everyone into the chapel. There are no seats, only the small altar, so it'll be fine. Just stay calm throughout. I know this is tough for you, Mum, and Dempsey.'

'You sure you're okay?'

Harry looked at me straight in the eye and said, 'Yes, I'm fine. This was meant to happen for a reason. It shows how popular Laura was. She was liked and loved by many. This is fate, Jack. But I believe that the Lord will look down on the righteous ones among us. He knows we are trying to do the right thing here. Keep believing. All right?'

'Okay, Harry. Thanks.'

We said nothing for a few seconds, then Harry put his arm around me. He didn't need to say anything else. As we waited by the car, Dempsey and Richard arrived with Mum, and came towards us.

Knowing the order we were to carry Laura in, we slid her out of the car, with Harry and I taking either side of the front of the coffin. We turned away from the car, towards the chapel entrance, walking slowly.

We went inside; it was empty other than us. Shortly after we'd set her down, it started to fill up quickly, with the local vicar ushering everyone in before finally closing the doors.

Harry took his place at the altar. I remembered very little about the service, other than standing next to Mum, feeling numb, wanting it to be over as quickly as possible.

I couldn't recall anything Harry said at all, as my mind drifted into my own memories of Laura. How we met, our first kiss, falling in love, working together in the shop, setting up home in the flat, our holidays, and finally, when everything had changed seven days ago. Harry did the service, and I made a speech all about Laura, telling everyone about all the things we'd done together. Fortunately, I had it all written down and knowing what was coming, managed to avoid breaking down completely in front of everyone, though I knew my voice was wavering enormously as I tried to control my emotions.

When it was over, I was the first one outside, wanting fresh air. Lots of people came up to me, some of whom I had no idea who they were.

'Lovely service,' said an old lady. I recognised her, as the lady from the train station. She was the grandmother of the boy Laura had saved, Tommy Jacobs.

'Thank you,' I replied.

'Wonderful young woman,' said a young lady to me. I didn't know her at first, until she told me her name. She continued to say, 'I went to school with Laura, you probably don't remember me, Jack? I moved away. I'm Daphne Jackson. We were best friends at school. I'm so sorry. If I can help with anything, let me know.'

'Thanks, Daphne, that's very kind of you,' I replied, as she leant forward to hug me, then kiss my cheek. I saw tears in her eyes.

I continued to shake hands with people, some I knew, some I didn't, and it merged into a blur for about half an hour.

Harry came over, joining Mum and I after speaking with the resident vicar. Dempsey was deep in conversation with Richard Leonard, no doubt talking about antiques, I thought, as well as Laura.

Eventually, everyone other than Richard left. He and Dempsey walked towards us. I felt torn apart, wanting to tell Richard what we had planned. But it wasn't possible. It would have jeopardised everything.

'Jack. I can only say again how sorry I am. Mary, it's tragic. If there's anything that I can ever do for you, don't hesitate to let me know.'

'Thank you, Richard.' Mum said. We were silent for a few moments and then she continued, 'Well, there may be something you could help with, actually, Richard.'

We all froze as she said this. Surely she wasn't going to tell him what we were about to try and do?

'Just ask away, Mary.'

Harry, Dempsey, and myself gave each other a quick glance, and I grabbed Mum's arm tightly, not knowing what she was going to say.

'Because of this situation, we have a great deal of stock—well Jack and Laura have—to dispose of. And a shop, too. Jack, we've talked about this already, so I hope you don't mind me saying this.'

We hadn't talked. Now I was getting jittery.

Mum smiled then—and I eased my grip on her arm— as I stood, open mouthed, not knowing if she was going to spill the beans about our plan. What was she going to say?

'Richard, as you are a very old and close friend of ours, would you be interested in purchasing the stock and shop? I know Jack feels like he needs a fresh start. Isn't that right, Jack?'

Still a bit shocked, I managed to say, 'Er, well. It's what Laura would've wanted, Mum. What do you think, Richard?'

'Give me a couple of days to think about it Jack, it's a big decision. You know I've got my shop in London, but I know your business is growing thanks to the internet, so it would be churlish of me not to give it serious consideration.'

Dempsey was just staring at me and Mum. He was lost for words right now.

'Food for thought, everyone,' said Harry. 'Now, if you don't mind, Richard, we're going to have a private mass ourselves. Sorry, but we'd planned originally for just a small service, none of us realised that there would be so many people here.'

'That's fine, Harry. Very nice to finally meet you, sadly in these circumstances.'

'Thanks, Richard. Good to meet you too.'

They shook hands and nodded to each other. Then Richard hugged Mum, Dempsey, and myself. I felt that he should be with us, being an old friend, but it could jeopardise everything. Still, he may be helping out by taking the business on instead, I thought.

As he turned, walking away from the chapel, I looked at Mum.

'That was a bit off the cuff, wasn't it? Blimey, Mum, I didn't know what you were going to say then.'

'Sorry. It's just that I know you'll need to get away from here, if and when this works. Now come on, all of you, we've not got a lot of time left. The evening is drawing in and it'll be dark soon.'

'Yep, you're right, Mum. Now, let's all get back into the chapel. To Laura,' Harry said. 'We've work to do still. Can you wait here by the entrance, please?' He looked at Mum whilst putting his arm around her. 'Jack, Dempsey, and I will go inside and wait for night to fall, so we need you to keep an eye out for the vicar, though he shouldn't be around now. I've got the keys to lock up.'

We went back into the chapel together, whilst Mum waited at the entrance door, keeping a watchful eye. We stood silently over the coffin, knowing we would have been due to take her to the burial plot. But that wasn't what we were going to do at all. As the dimming light began to fade outside, Harry and I eased the lid off the coffin.

A few minutes later, with darkness falling, we were ready. Time to carry Laura out of the chapel, around to the shrine outside. There was just the three of us this time, though it wasn't heavy at all. Lifting the coffin up, we carried her at waist height, instead of putting her on our shoulders as before. Silently, and slowly, we walked around to the shrine, with Mum following us. She had the stones with her.

11. The shrine.

When we arrived at the shrine, it was as I'd seen it before with Harry. A concrete plinth about four feet high, the size of a small grave, with a statue of St. Augustine at one end. It was hidden away by bushes and trees, in a private area. That, we already knew, would help us.

We put Laura on top of the shrine in silence in the now open-topped coffin. I felt suddenly aware of the cold evening air.

'It'd better work, Jack. Remember what I said to you,' said Dempsey quietly to me, so that Mum and Harry couldn't hear.

But Mum heard him. 'Dempsey, have faith now. My sons believe. So thank you for being here. We all know how hard this is for you. For all of us.'

He stared at Mum. Just stared at her, saying nothing more. There was silence for a few seconds before Harry spoke.

'Put the stones in place, Mum. Jack and I will be here next to you.'

'Now, I need you all to be quiet. I know it's cold. But silence is needed for the incantations,' instructed Mum.

She placed the three stones on top of Laura's fully clothed body, one each on her neck, chest, and waist. I looked at my watch; it was almost seven p.m. It was a few hours until midnight, but not much time left to bring her back, I thought.

Dempsey was standing on his own on one side of the shrine, whilst Harry and I stood either side of Mum.

She began to whisper. I couldn't hear what she was saying. Her voice was too quiet. Then, it became louder, but still I didn't understand. I could make out the odd word, which I vaguely recognised as Gaelic. After a few minutes, she began to almost whisper the words once again.

With Mum still chanting quietly, I could see the three stones glowing on top of Laura. They stayed a bright green colour for about one minute. I didn't take my eyes off Laura's face for a second.

Mum finally stopped chanting and when she did, that's when it happened.

The shrine was bathed in a bright white light, which appeared from nowhere. It shone straight out of the sky, from the darkness up above, into the coffin, immersing Laura fully. The light was blinding. After a few seconds, it vanished as quickly as it had appeared.

Then we heard it.

Thunder like I'd never heard before in my life, followed by lightning. It only lasted for a few seconds, but lit the sky up all around us. No rain came. Just several claps of thunder with bolts of lightning, which crashed around the ground where we stood.

Then, silence, other than Mum continuing chanting, uttering some words that I understood. So must've Harry and Dempsey, as all three of us stared at her when the lightning ceased, as she shouted, 'Sacrifice. I agree. Sacrifice. I agree!'

I glanced at Dempsey, then Harry. We were all open-mouthed with disbelief, staring at Mum. She was in a trance like state, it seemed.

She gave a gasp and cried out 'YES!', then fell backwards, with Harry catching her just before her limp body crashed to the ground. She'd collapsed, luckily, into his arms. I thought maybe he'd expected it.

As Harry held her, I quickly went to them to see if Mum was okay. I feared the worst, that we'd lost her and Laura. Had it all been a tragic failure? But Mum was breathing, I could see that, and the panic I felt subsided.

Then, I left her to see if Laura had come back. No movement, nothing. What had we done? I thought I'd lost her forever now. I stared at her, willing her to wake up. There was an eerie silence, other than the wind blowing around the trees for a few moments, before I spoke.

'Harry? What's going on? It hasn't worked!' I shouted.

'Wait. Just wait, Jack. You too, Dempsey. It needs time.'

'What the hell is going on, Harry?' shouted Dempsey.

'I said wait! Please,' shouted Harry.

We waited in silence for a few seconds before I lost the plot completely.

'It hasn't bloody worked! It's all been for nothing. Now I'll never get her back!' I shouted, with rage and anger in my voice, directed at Harry and Mum.

Harry cradled Mum in his arms, and as she started to come back round, he looked up at me before speaking.

'I said wait, Jack! It's not finished yet!'

'Help me up, Harry. Now! I've got to see her,' said Mum

'Are you okay, Mum?' Harry replied. I was dumbstruck for a moment, frozen, not knowing what to do, or if it had worked.

'Yes, but it's not finished yet, you know that. I need to touch her.'

Harry helped Mum to her feet, as she leant forward to touch Laura on her forehead with her own hand.

'Sacrifice. Yes. I agree.' That's all Mum said again, quietly.

Within a second, she was in a daze again, but this time she didn't faint or collapse. Harry was holding her close to keep her on her feet. They both took a step backwards from where Laura lay, inside the coffin, still not moving.

There was silence for what seemed like an eternity, but was merely a few seconds.

As Harry held Mum, I leant over the coffin towards Laura's face, hoping and praying that she would wake up.

Then it happened. I heard a gasp. Slowly, Laura's eyes opened. Then, she forced out the first words I'd heard since that day at the station on the platform. 'Jack. Oh, Jack!'

She was alive. *Laura was alive!*

I put my hands inside the coffin, embracing her. She put her hands up to my face and touched my cheek. Amazingly, her hands were warm. Pulling herself towards me, she kissed me. It was incredible. It had worked. It had really worked. Laura was back!

Looking at each other as she lay in the coffin, we smiled at each other. I never thought I'd see that smile again. Now I wanted it to remain on her face forever.

'Oh, Jack. I could hear your mother praying for me every day,' she said, her voice sounding stronger, almost like it had been before.

Dempsey stood staring, open-mouthed, as I glanced up at him whilst holding onto Laura tightly. I turned my head towards Harry, who was still holding Mum; they were both smiling at us. *We did it*, I thought to myself. I could feel the tears on my own face again, I was so happy.

I put my arms under Laura's waist and legs. As I did so, the stones fell from her body into the coffin, the colour now gone from them. Lifting Laura out, still carrying her, we kissed as I held her close to my body. I couldn't quite believe it was all real.

'Is this real, Jack?' said Laura. 'And Dad, without you this wouldn't have been possible. I know that. I could hear you, all the time. It was like I was in a deep, deep sleep. How can I ever thank you? And Harry. You too.' She was crying now too, sobbing almost uncontrollably as I held her tightly in my arms.

'Glad you're back, Laura. I knew it was possible, as did Mum. Jack has been beside himself, but not now, eh brother?'

'Not now,' I said, knowing I was smiling as I spoke. 'I can't believe what you've all done. This feels like it's truly a miracle.'

'Well, not far from it brother,' said Harry, still holding onto Mum, supporting her.

'Well, I'm very tired, Jack, and need to rest,' said Mum. 'This has been a long few days. Can you boys get us all out of here? Let's get back to the cottage as soon as possible.'

Laura slipped out of my embrace, and I gently let her slide out of my arms so that she could stand up. She instantly hugged Mum. Neither of them said anything. They didn't need to as they stared at each other, smiling, with tears in both of their eyes. We all stood silently for a few moments, knowing it'd actually worked.

Breaking the silence, Laura said, whilst still embracing Mum, 'How can I—we—ever thank you for this? We owe you everything. Thank you, again.'

Still holding Laura, Mum said, 'Live, Laura. Just live. Be happy with Jack. That's all I ask.' Then they both smiled at each other before Mum continued. 'We'd better get going, you lot.' Nobody answered her, but Harry and I nodded to each other, knowing what we had to do next.

***

The funeral cars had gone, but we'd already planned to leave our old car here this morning, so we'd be able to drive home together, all five of us.

But before that, we had to dispose of the coffin. We'd arranged for a burial plot, which we now had to fill. Plus we'd got some bricks and soil ready to put inside to give it some weight.

Quickly, we walked to the car, leaving Mum and Laura together inside it. Then we went back to collect the coffin and lid, to take to the plot, where we put it in place ourselves, covering it over with soil. Mum had already collected her three stones herself and had them with her in the car. They'd stopped glowing earlier when the thunder and lightning had finished.

Once we'd finished filling in the grave, we returned to the car as quickly as possible. Nobody else was around.

Getting back to the car, I sat in the driver's seat. Mum was sitting in the back with Laura, and Dempsey had joined them. Harry jumped into the front seat next to me. He'd locked up the chapel. I wanted to hold Laura now, but knew it wouldn't be long before I could again.

'Right, back to the cottage then,' I said.

'But I need to drop these keys off first, Jack.'

'Oh, er, okay.'

'Bloody marvellous!' shouted Harry, completely out of character, as he never swore. 'Welcome back Laura.'

I looked in the rear-view mirror, seeing Mum, Laura and Dempsey all smiling.

I pulled away from the chapel, down the winding road, thinking about all we'd been through. It felt surreal, almost like being in another world. But it wasn't, it was real. I smiled to myself as I checked the rear mirror again, seeing Mum and Laura holding each other. It was difficult holding onto the excitement that I felt inside. I wanted to shout out to the world about what had happened. But I knew that wasn't possible.

After a short drive, Harry dropped the keys off at the vicar's house, then we drove home, all quiet in the car. Mum was almost asleep in the backseat, still holding Laura tightly. I saw Laura glance at her Dad, smiling at him. He smiled back. We'd done it. She really was back.

Arriving at Mum's cottage, we all went straight indoors, not wanting to be seen by anybody. Now that Laura was back, we really had to make plans to go away for good. No one would believe that she'd come back from the dead.

'Boys, I'm very tired. I'm going to have a lie down on my bed. Laura, I love you. Always have. This would've never worked for anyone other than you. You know that, don't you?' said Mum.

'Yes, Mother. I know. And I wouldn't be here if not for you. Thank you. Thank you so, so much. I love you too.'

Then they hugged again before Mum made her way upstairs. But as she did, I said, 'What was the sacrifice about Mum? What did it mean?'

'Let me sleep, Jack. I'll tell you in the morning. I'm just so tired right now.'

'Okay. Have a good sleep.'

She went upstairs, seeming and looking weary, more so than I'd ever seen her before.

'Harry, what's the sacrifice mean? You know, don't you?' I questioned.

'Well, I've got an idea, but I'm not completely sure. Wait until Mum wakes later, or in the morning, and we'll find out then. Right now, you've Laura to think about.'

He was right. I did have Laura to think about, as I turned towards her, forgetting about the sacrifice thing, hoping we would have each other for a long, long time.

Laura was sitting with Dempsey on the settee. They were holding hands. I stared over at them. She seemed slightly pale now, as if she had been drained by the whole event.

'You feeling okay, Laura?' I said, as I walked over to her and bent down on my knees in front of her, taking her hands in mine.

'Feeling a bit faint, actually. Not surprised really, with everything I've been through.' She smiled at me, and I smiled back.

'Time to rest before we make plans,' I said, standing back up again.

'What plans are they, Jack?'

'Well, with you back, it's a case of having to. Don't forget, you passed away in my arms just a week ago. We've had a funeral for you. Now you've returned. I want to shout it from the rooftops, to tell everyone. But I can't. To stay here isn't possible. The whole world would want to know how and why. So, we've no choice. Sorry, baby. It's the only way.'

'What d'you think, Dad?'

'He's right, Laura. It's the only way. You've to stay in the cottage until Jack's organised everything. He can tell you where you're going, to start your life over again. Together.'

'Where to, Jack?'

'Hold it one moment, all of you. I've got something else to tell you,' said Harry. 'This is to do with your return, Laura. Jack, this is the most wonderful gift ever. Dempsey, I know you've not fully agreed, but it's happened. There's no choice other than to start afresh elsewhere. Sorry, but that's the only way. But, after Mum's help, I know from The Book of Scrolls that it's not over yet.'

'What do you mean, Harry? My daughter's here now. I can see her. I can touch her.'

'What Mum doesn't know from the readings is that there are now seven more days to wait until Laura returns fully.'

'How come you know and Mary doesn't?' Dempsey said, raising his voice.

'Well, you know I've been studying the book for some time as part of my priesthood. Some things Mum can't understand, because that knowledge can only be gained by conversations with the elders; they know more about the book than anyone else on the planet. Stories have been passed down through the generations which have never been written. It's just fortunate that I've been at my seminary, where the original book is kept. That's how I've got more in-depth knowledge than anyone else.'

'So, why another seven days, Harry?' I asked.

'Simple really. It's seven more days, just like the seven it took to create life. These seven days are for Laura to get back her life. There is a possibility that she may change, but that's only a small possibility.'

'What do you mean by change?' I questioned.

'Jack, the readings only say that there's a second seven days to get through, before returning fully formed, if one stone is missing. I've got some more reading to do, and have to get back to Ireland to finish off some questions with the elders.'

'Are you joking? After going through all of this, it mightn't be over yet?' I shouted at him.

'Sorry, Jack. I knew timing was everything, but at least this way, we have seven more days to find out if we need to do anything else.'

'Come on, Harry! I don't believe this. She's here. It's real enough.'

'I know, but I've got to make sure that it's for good. You can see how pale Laura is. I think this is a temporary state due to the missing fourth stone.'

'This is crazy. It's as bad as when Mum first told me this.'

There was stunned silence. Then Dempsey spoke. 'I told you, Jack. I'm holding you responsible!' He leapt from the settee, lunging at me. Harry stood in front of me and took the brunt of the attack, getting knocked over.

'Stop, Dempsey! Stop!' I shouted, and he backed off. 'This isn't doing any good at all. Harry's the one who knows what to do. I think its madness too, but we've got to listen to him. He's given me—us—time.'

'You mark my words, I'm holding you accountable, Jack Stanton! You alone. I told you before, only a few days ago, about the implications of Laura roaming the earth. Now it's a possibility. This has opened a gateway between heaven and earth, and for all we know, hell too! I want no more part of it. I did this to help under duress, you know that! I'm sorry, Laura.' He stared at her, before continuing. 'You have to stay here, Laura. It's the only way. I'm going back to the house. You'll be safe here for now, I know that. I know you love her Jack, but you know my concerns. Harry, I'm disappointed in you for not knowing the full facts about what could happen. And your mother, Mary, also knowing what could happen. I can't stand to be here any longer. I've got to go. Laura, I spoke to Jack a couple of days ago, telling him how dangerous I thought this was. Now, it's not over. It's dragging on and I don't know where you'll end up. You could be roaming the earth as a spirit instead of resting in peace, thanks to you all, and your foolish old mother! But remember Jack, I told you about good and evil. You alone are responsible.'

He walked out of our cottage then, with anger and hatred in his face, directed towards me. There was a stunned silence then, until Harry spoke; he'd now got himself up from the floor. 'Hey Jack, it'll be okay. I'm going back to Ireland to check the original book and talk to the elders. We'll find a way within a week, if we need it.'

Just then, I turned to look at Laura. She was staring open-mouthed with wide eyes; her father had tried to attack me and had stormed out of the cottage. But she looked pale, even more so than before, with a shocked look on her face, teary eyed and with a trembling lower lip. I reached out to her and held her in my arms as she sobbed quietly. I looked at Harry, before he spoke.

'Jack, listen. It's happening. I'm sorry. You can see how pale Laura is. That means she's fading. We've got seven days, from the moment she returned this evening. I only know from my readings that she's going to look transparent on and off until... until... I don't know when. I've got to translate the book, Jack!'

'God, this is a mess, Harry. Mum's exhausted, Laura's fading, Dempsey's wild with fury. Now you've got to get back to Ireland to try and translate the original book. What the hell am I going to do now?'

'Make plans, Jack. You know where you've got to go. A fresh start. New York, maybe. This could be linked to the missing fourth stone fragment. That's my guess. I don't know that for a fact yet, but give me a couple of days to get back and I'll know. Start making plans. Get on with it. You've no choice.'

'I know you're right. I've always trusted you. But is this a step too far?'

'No, it's not. Never think like that. It'll work out. Don't waver, brother, keep your faith true and strong.'

'Okay. Okay.'

Laura was still in my arms, with her head resting on my shoulder, watching and listening to us. I glanced at her and could see her pale features. She, too, looked very tired.

'Now, take Laura to bed, to our old room upstairs. Mum's probably asleep already. We need to sleep, as well, we've still got a lot to do.' Harry said.

I stared at him. Despite the desperate situation we were in, I still trusted him with my life. And Laura's now, too.

So I carried her upstairs, as she was now almost fast asleep, exhausted by her ordeal. Tucking her into bed, I kissed her goodnight. It was getting late. So, we'd got through day seven. She was back. As I stroked her hair, I knew that we only had seven more days from now—again—to save her permanently. I desperately wanted to lie down with Laura, but she was so drained I left her there to sleep. I put my face close to hers, just to check that she was still breathing, which she was. I kissed her soft cheek as she slept and crept out of the room.

I looked in on Mum. She'd fallen asleep on top of her own bed, so I pulled the covers around her. She barely moved and looked exhausted, as well. We'd been through a lot these past few days. We all needed to sleep. I hoped Dempsey was all right. I went back downstairs; Harry had fallen asleep in the armchair, so I plonked myself on the settee, where I began to fall asleep within minutes myself.

12. Mum's sacrifice.

When I finally awoke the next morning, I still had my suit on from the funeral. Harry was still asleep in the armchair opposite me. No sign of Mum or Laura, they must've been asleep still, I thought. I'd been so tired, I'd slept well.

Getting up, I went straight upstairs to check on Laura and Mum.

Going into the bedroom, I saw Laura, still fast asleep. She still looked pale, almost translucent. That was worrying. But she was here. So, I left her to sleep.

Next, I popped into Mum's bedroom. She was awake—just.

'Hey Mum, you okay?'

'I'm fine, Jack. And you? I've had one of the best sleeps ever, feels like I've been asleep for ten years.'

'Mum, you look different. You all right?'

'Bit achy all over, but other than that, good. Who put the covers over me, you?'

'Yep, I did. Well, I'll leave you to get yourself up and about, I'll go and put the kettle on. Laura's still asleep. And Dempsey stormed off last night. Blames me for everything.'

'Why didn't you wake me? I could've spoken to him.'

'No point. His mind's made up, thinks we've gone against God's holy law, and like I said, he says it's my fault and he's holding me accountable. Um, it's likely that Laura's only got seven days with us, as it's temporary. Harry's got to find out some more information from the elders at the seminary in Ireland.'

'What? I knew he had to get some more information, but not this. Surely not?'

'Mum, I trust Harry. Always have. He's never let me down since we were kids. I know he's been away, but he's always been there for me. So, get yourself sorted and come downstairs when you're ready, I'll make us a nice cuppa—not one of your herbal teas this time. I'll leave Laura until she stirs from her slumber.'

'All right, I'll be down in a few minutes.'

True to her word, it was a matter of minutes. As I came back down the stairs, Harry was stirring in the armchair. As I walked into the living room, he got up from the chair, stretching his arms into the air, touching the low cottage ceiling.

'Tea, Harry?'

'Yep, please. But not one of those herbal ones Mum likes, I can't get on with them.'

'Acquired taste, I think. Only just got used to them myself recently.'

We both walked into the kitchen. Neither of us had washed and I could see his hair was a mess, sticking up all over the place from falling asleep the night before.

'I've got to organise a flight to Ireland right away, Jack. I'll get onto it now.'

'But have a shower first, and a change of clothes, Harry.'

He looked at the crumpled priest regalia he was still wearing, checking the little mirror in the kitchen.

'Hmm. You've got a point there. While that kettle's on I'll go up and get changed. Have a quick shower.'

'I'll have one after you. Can you check on Mum while you're up there, she said she'd be a few minutes and be down here.'

As I said that, she came into the kitchen.

'I heard you, Jack. My tea ready yet?'

Harry and I looked at each other. She'd had a quick shower, and got dressed. But she looked different. As we stared at each other, the kettle boiled, and Harry said, 'Mum, I think it's happened.'

'I know, Harry. You'd better explain to your brother and Laura when she's awake.'

'Explain what?' I said.

'I'll go and wake Laura, Jack. You need to hear this together,' Mum replied.

She went back upstairs to go and wake Laura. I just looked at Harry. We both knew already that Mum had aged.

'Harry, she's got grey hair. And her face has got wrinkles overnight. What the hell is going on here?'

'Wait until Laura's here. I'll tell you together.'

We went into the living room with our drinks, waited for a couple of minutes, then Mum returned, with Laura following behind her. She came straight over and kissed me, holding me tightly.

'Just want to say I love you. I'll say that every day now for the rest of our lives, Jack.' Then she looked at Mum with a quizzical stare. She could see she'd changed.

'And I love you too, baby,' I whispered into her ear. 'Think you'd better sit down, Harry's got something important to tell us. Haven't you, Harry?' I said this louder, so that they'd all hear me.

'Yes. Laura, please sit down. You too, Jack.'

'Sounds ominous, doesn't it, Jack?' Laura said light-heartedly.

'Think it is,' I replied in a more serious tone.

We sat on the settee together. Harry was standing, and Mum sat in the armchair.

'We've got you back Laura,' continued Harry. 'But— and I'll take this slowly—we've got you here for seven days only. If you look at your skin you can see it's pale. That, I know now, is a temporary state for you. Don't panic and don't worry. I think I know how to put it right.'

'Don't worry? Harry, I feel fine. Tired, but otherwise fine.'

'Yes, I understand that. What we've done is to get you a temporary seven days. I think I know from the book, what I've to do. Jack knows that through my readings and conversations with the elders at the seminary, we've got something missing. I'm pretty sure I know what it is. But I need to confirm it with the elders myself.'

'What is it, Harry? You've got to tell us!' said Laura.

'Well, Mum's got three of the four stones. It's the missing fourth stone. That's what I think we need. Well, I know it's what we need now. But exactly what it'll do and if there's anything else, I need to check in the book with the elders; they're the only ones that'll know.'

'So go! Get over there. This is day one of seven all over again. And we've got to go and find that stone, haven't we? I remember you said it went to a museum years ago. Mum said you know where. Well, do you, Harry?' I said.

'I think so. I'll get a flight as soon as I can and call you from the seminary. This'll work out, just give me a couple of days.'

'That's about all we can give you, Harry. We'll be waiting for you to return. I'll speak to Dempsey in the meantime, try and calm him down.'

'Right o then. I'll get onto the airport now. But before that, I've got to tell you about Mum.' The room went silent for a moment before Harry continued. 'So, Mum. Before we started, we spoke about this, didn't we?'

'Yes, we did. Go ahead, you've to tell them now, Harry.'

There was another silence as we waited for Harry to tell us what had happened to Mum.

'Okay. When I first looked at the book, and the implications, it mentioned a sacrifice to pay. The person undertaking the task—Mum—has a price to pay. At first, I couldn't understand what that was. But before I came over, a couple of days after the train accident, I worked out what it was.'

'What, Harry?' I questioned.

'It's time, Jack. The person who undertakes the task can only be one of the seventh born of the seventh born. That is, Dempsey or Mum. We knew that Dempsey wouldn't do this because of his concerns. So, it could only be Mum. She knew the incantations required in the Gaelic language, but not about the time factor.'

'Time? But what do you mean by time?' queried Laura.

Harry continued. 'It turned out to be a simple translation. When this act is complete, time will be taken as a sacrifice from the person who has undertaken it. Obviously, that's Mum.' There was a deafening silence. Nobody spoke for a few seconds before Harry continued. 'She will age. The time taken is the age you are now, Laura, being twenty-five. That will be added to Mum's life, so within the next seven days she will age twenty-five years. It was the only way possible.'

There was another stunned silence in the room.

I looked over at Mum. I knew already. Harry and I had seen her this morning, with her slightly greying hair. It wasn't fair. I hadn't known.

'Mum. You never said what this would do to you. Why? You should've said.'

'Jack, it's okay. I wanted to do this. I've still got time on my side. I'm forty-seven now, so going up to seventy-two I can accept, knowing that you and Laura have a chance of a life together. It's a one off. But I wanted to do this for you both,' Mum said, through teary eyes and with a broken, stuttering voice.

We sat silently again. Laura started to cry. I had tears in my eyes now, not knowing what else to say.

After a few moments, Laura went to Mum and embraced her. They both cried, holding each other, saying nothing, until Laura spoke.

'Thank you. I don't know how I can ever repay you.'

'No need. I always knew that this may happen. But I could only ever do this for one person. That's you, Laura. Don't ask me to explain why, I just knew. Just live long and be very happy.'

'Mum?' I said. But before I could continue, she spoke.

'Listen. I did this because there's a chance for you two to have a long and happy life together. You do deserve it. There is much I could say, but there's no need now. The deed is done, and it's what I wanted to do. Please say no more about this. Be there for me. I know I'm going to age, but I'm prepared for it. I've already had a good life. Now, let's get organised, there's a lot to do, all of you.'

There was a lot to do.

And this was a sacrifice she was prepared to make for us. How could I ever repay her? How could we ever thank her?

13. Journalist's intervention.

We sat around the cottage that day and the next, because Harry couldn't get a flight until the late evening of day two. We discussed what we would need to do while Harry was away, and afterwards, if it all worked out. In the meantime, I knew I had to go and speak to Dempsey. Without Laura.

She couldn't leave the house for fear of being seen.

The time came to take Harry for his flight. Our trust and faith was with him now and it was being fully tested. We needed the other stone. Only he could know what to do when we found it.

I drove back from the airport in the early hours of the morning, on what was now the third day of seven, hoping to get some sleep before going to see Dempsey later that morning.

I slept on the settee so as not to disturb Laura and Mum, leaving them sleeping. I woke to go to Dempsey's later that morning, going to see Laura upstairs before I left.

'Jack, don't agitate him, please?' she said, with sleepy eyes.

'No, of course not. But you know his state of mind right now. I'll be back soon, tell you about it then, okay?'

'Okay.' We kissed, and I left. It was nine thirty in the morning now, and I hoped he'd be up by the time I got there.

Arriving at Dempsey's house, I knocked on his front door. No answer. I walked round to the back door, but could see nobody in. I tried his mobile phone. No answer again, so I left a voicemail message for him.

Going back to the cottage, there was nothing I could do but wait. I'd try and get hold of Dempsey again later today, or tomorrow. It'd be a couple of days before Harry returned so I had time; although now I knew that Mum didn't have the time we had.

He didn't return my call that day, so I decided to wait until the next day to go and see him.

At around lunchtime the following day, I went to Dempsey's house again. I could see he was in as there were lights on in the living room. It was another dull day in mid-January. It would've only been a few more days and Laura and I would have been getting married, I thought to myself.

Knocking on the door, I waited for Dempsey to answer. I could hear the stomp of feet approaching from inside. Then the door opened.

'Hey Jack, how're you doing?'

'I'm fine. And you? I came round after taking Harry to the airport yesterday, but you were out.'

'Broke the golden rule, Jack. Went out and got hammered. Didn't expect to see you for a few days. What do you want?' he said in a sullen and forceful tone.

I knew by the way he was talking that he was getting over a hangover right now, as well as holding onto his own anger.

'Do you fancy a coffee then, after your session last night?'

'I s'pose so,' he replied loudly.

'I'll stick the kettle on, if you let me in.'

'Yep, come in, Jack. I may be sick of the sight of you all, but I'd like to know how you're going to get out of this mess. You know what I said. My daughter's likely to end up roaming around as a lost soul or spirit. It's God damned ridiculous. We should never have done this!'

'Shall I come in Dempsey, before you shout out to the whole of the road and town what we've done?'

'Okay. Okay. Get in and put that kettle on,' he replied, in a slightly quieter and calmer voice.

I walked through to the kitchen, putting the kettle on. Dempsey was still in a dressing gown and went upstairs, I presumed to put some clothes on.

Ten minutes later, he came back down after getting dressed.

'Right, what're you planning on doing with my daughter now?' he shouted.

'Look. There's no need for the animosity, I know you blame me for all of this. I get that. But we're trying to get her back for good.'

'Not much chance of that! You're just as crazy as your mum and brother. The stupid, silly Stanton family you all are. Huh!'

'Oh, come on! As if you weren't a part of this too! You had your doubts, we all knew that. But for Christ's sake, Dempsey, Laura's back now! We've got time to try and keep her forever. Don't you want to help anymore?'

'Think I've done enough helping already, don't you?'

I stood silently, watching him as he sipped the coffee I'd made him. I still couldn't dislike him. He'd been so kind and generous towards Laura and myself. I waited for him to continue.

'And another thing,' Dempsey said, 'I went out last night. Went to one of the local bars. That was after I'd downed the rest of that half a bottle of scotch I didn't have, when you asked me to stop drinking a few days ago.'

'So, seems like it helped you then, seeing as you reeked of booze when I came in.'

'Hmm. Well. I spoke to a couple of the guys in the bar. One of them was a journalist, you know. And there's something else you should know too, Jack!' Dempsey said with a wry, smirk.

'And what's that?'

Dempsey was getting louder again, and angrier. Knowing this could turn ugly like the other evening at the cottage, I sat down in his kitchen, gesturing for him to join me. I thought it'd be easier, and calmer, if we sat down to talk. Fortunately, he sat down, before continuing and telling me what had happened.

'Well. I sat at the bar having a pint, and one of the guys is a regular there. His name's Will Jacobs, and he's the dad of that little lad Laura saved the life of at the train station,' he said, in a much calmer tone.

'Really? And what did you say to him?'

'Bet you didn't know that he's a journalist, Jack. And it was his mother who was with his little boy, Tommy, the day Laura saved him. How about that for a coincidence, hmm?'

'Well, I suppose it's coincidental, yes.'

'He knew me, as he went to the funeral to pay his respects. He bought me a couple of drinks to say how sorry he was that my daughter Laura had died saving his boy. Nice bloke, that Will Jacobs.'

'And was that it? He thanked you in his own way?'

'Not exactly, Jack. I've left the best bit until last.'

'That is?'

'Huh. Now I've sobered up a bit, I can remember what I said to him. And you won't like it m'boy.'

'Come on then, you're itching to tell me, so spill the beans!'

'Laura's alive! That's what I told him. And I said she's been reborn and is staying at your Mum's cottage. Everyone knows her in our community, it's not a big town, Jack. And what's more, I think he believed me!'

'No! What the hell did you do that for?'

'Because it's wrong. You know what I think. And I was getting blind drunk at the time. And I'm not sorry I told him either!'

'Stupid! You're so stupid, Dempsey. Drink more coffee, get sobered up properly. You've ruined everything now. What the hell were you thinking? I've told you there's a chance to bring her back properly, now you've jeopardised that. Idiot!'

'Nothing to do now but wait for his story to explode, eh?'

'You don't know what you've done! And you don't know what happened after you stormed out of the cottage either!'

'Oh? Not another revelation, surely.'

'Wasn't that. But something awful. And it doesn't affect Laura, by the way. I know you've always cared for my mum. But now, when I tell you what happened, you mightn't feel so smug.'

He stared at me. I could see confusion in his face. I'd known he'd always liked Mum, and I'd hit a raw nerve.

'What?'

I stood up from my chair. Rage was inside me now. I grabbed his shirt and pulled him out of his chair. Pushing him against kitchen cupboards, I put my face so close to his, I could feel his breath on me.

'My mother has sacrificed herself to give your daughter life! That's what! For Laura to come back, she will age. When these seven days are past, she'll have taken the twenty-five years Laura's had already. And furthermore, it's started already! Happy now?'

I let go of him. He stared at me. Just stared at me. My anger subsided as I sat back down again, putting my head in my hands, tears welling up in my eyes.

'Jack. Son. I'm sorry.' I could hear remorse in his voice now.

Looking up at him, I said nothing. What could I say now? He knew about my mum. He blamed me still, but she was the one who'd made the sacrifice.

'I'll think of something to put the journalist guy off the scent. You're right, I'm an idiot. I've been thinking too much of myself and Laura, of course. I can tell him I made it up.'

I looked at him, staring into his eyes. He seemed a broken man now.

'Oh God! And I said she was a silly old woman the other night, as well. This is terrible. How can I get you and her to forgive me?'

Sitting in silence, I had no idea what we'd do to get this journalist off our backs now. Dempsey paced around in the kitchen for a minute or so.

'Got it!' shouted Dempsey.

I just looked at him, shrugged my shoulders, not expecting anything useful from him.

'You get back to the cottage. I'm not saying I agree with all of this, but I've got an idea, Jack. Laura's at the cottage, right?'

'Yep, you know she's staying there until Harry returns from Ireland.'

'Right then. Get back over there. The journalist guy said he'd come and see me today, wanted some more information about Laura. He thought I was a bit crazy—which I was—when I told him about Laura coming back. All I said was that she'd been reborn and had returned. But, when he turns up later today, I'll tell him that it's Laura's long lost sister who's back.'

'What?'

'Listen, Jack. Phone your mum now. Get her to put some make-up on Laura if she's still pale, and you get back there. I'll bring the guy over with me if he wants to see Laura. We'll tell him that she's her sister. She didn't make the funeral in time, but she's staying over with you for a few days until she goes back to Australia. I can make it all up, Jack. I want to help, now I've cocked up the situation and know about your mother.'

'This is ridiculous. But I know we've got no choice.'

'No, we haven't now, thanks to my stupidity. You told me before about drinking, Jack. I did stop before, and this was my one indiscretion. I'm truly sorry.'

We were still standing in the kitchen, and he reached out to me, but didn't grab me aggressively like he'd done a few minutes before. He embraced me. After his anger, it wasn't what I'd expected from him. But, I was pleased just the same.

I looked him directly in the eyes then, as he eased his hold on me. 'Right. I'm going back to the cottage. I'll explain it all to them, while you wait for the journalist to turn up. Give me a call if you're coming over with him, as he's likely to want to verify this... this... story.'

'Thanks, Jack.'

I turned and walked straight into the hallway towards the front door, not bothering to say goodbye. Getting into the car, I was about to drive the couple of miles back to the cottage, forgetting to call. But, as I pulled away, I saw a car pull up in my rear view mirror outside Dempsey's house, as I turned the corner of his road. It had to be the journalist Will Jacobs, I thought.

Putting my foot down, I got back to the cottage as quickly as I could, to explain the plan to get rid of the journalist.

Ten minutes later, I was back at the cottage. Rushing inside, I found Mum and Laura sipping tea. I didn't have much time to get this plan sorted, I thought to myself.

'What's up, Jack?' said Mum.

'Didn't have time to call you both. Dempsey's coming over with a journalist. It's the boy's dad. You know, the kid whose life you saved, Laura, little Tommy Jacobs. His dad Will, is a journalist.'

'Why's he bringing him here?'

'Cockup by your Dad, Laura, I'm afraid.'

What d'you mean?'

'Well, last night, he went to one of the local bars and got blind drunk. He met a couple of guys, one being this Will Jacobs, who as I've said, is a journalist, of all things.'

'And don't tell me, he told him that Laura was still alive?'

'How'd you know that, Mum?'

'Doesn't matter how I know, Jack, I just do. So, what's our plan?'

'He's told Will that Laura's still alive, that she's been reborn. Stupid thing to do I know, but he was drunk, unfortunately.'

'So, what now then?' questioned Laura.

'We've concocted a plan, that you are actually Laura's long lost sister. Returned from Australia after being contacted by your dad, after the incident at the train station.'

'And why does he want to come here?' said Laura.

'Proof. Seeing as he'd been told that you're alive, and now he's just been told that you're a long lost sister, he's got the journalist bit between his teeth I reckon. Wants to know if you are Laura, or the sister.'

'And is Dempsey, bringing him over here soon?'

'Yes, Mum. I've just left him, to come and warn you both. Laura, we've got to try and make you look less pale. That'll be hard as you've come from Australia, and it's likely you should have a nice tan from the sun out there. Mum I need your help with make-up, please. A temporary tan for Laura, and maybe a couple of wrinkles if you can, so it looks like the sun has taken its toll on her face and hands, maybe.' I stopped talking and stared at them both before Mum took over.

'Let's get weaving then, the pair of you. Laura, upstairs now, please. Won't take too long. I've got some herbs that'll help with this too. And a hairpiece. You got a name yet for this sister, Jack?'

'Er, no actually. As I left his house I saw what I thought was the journalist's car pull up. Not spoken about a name yet. How about, er, Jeannie or Barbara?'

'Hmm, Barbara sounds good. You get that kettle on, Jack, I'll get Laura—I mean Barbara—fixed up with a tan and wrinkles.'

'Thanks, Mum.'

They went upstairs to transform Laura, whilst I went into the kitchen to try and keep calm, making myself a cup of tea. I checked my watch; it'd been about twenty minutes since I'd left Dempsey's house.

Shortly after Mum and Laura went upstairs, my mobile phone rang. It was Dempsey.

'Hello?'

'Hey, Jack. Are you at your Mum's cottage?'

'Yes, I am.' He knew I was, but I knew that he had company, so I played along.

'I've got someone who wants to come over, to check a story I told him last night in the bar.'

'Yep, sure. No problem. Who is he?'

'A guy named Will Jacobs. You remember the boy Tommy Jacobs, who Laura saved that day at the train station?'

'Er, yes.' I was slightly taken aback. It made me think of Laura lying on the station platform, dying.

'He wants to pop over to see Laura's sister. I told him last night that Laura was reborn. Sorry Jack, I was drunk as a skunk and talking gibberish to him in the bar.'

'That's all right. You come on over when you like. Your other daughter's here now.'

'Oh, Anne's there still, is she?' I could hear surprise in his voice when he said the name.

'Er, yes. Anne is. She's still here,' I said. He'd obviously given her a name already.

'Good. I'll be over with Mr Jacobs shortly, to meet her.'

'See you when you get here then. Thanks.'

He cut off his phone and I knew it'd only be about ten or fifteen minutes, no more than that, before he arrived.

'Mum, Dempsey's on his way with the little boy's dad. Feeling okay, the pair of you?' I shouted to them upstairs.

'Just coming down now,' shouted Laura.

A few moments later, they both appeared in the living room.

'Well, Jack. What do you think of my tan and the new wrinkles on my face and hands?'

I stared at Laura, smiling, before speaking. 'Nice work, Mum. She looks older now and not pasty and pale. And the blond wig looks good, too. No offence, Laura. And you're not Barbara or Jeannie. You've already been given a name by your dad. For now, when they turn up, you're Anne.'

We all laughed. But not for long. Just a few moments.

'Mum, you okay? I know what's happening to you. I'll never be able to thank you enough. Dempsey knows too. Couldn't believe what you've done for Laura, when I told him. That's why he decided to help get us out of this situation with Will Jacobs. He knows he's cocked-up big time. Just hope it works out.'

'It'll work, son. Now remember, for the next hour or so, this is Anne. Not Laura, but Anne. And she's come back from Australia for this sad occasion.'

'Fine, Mum. Thanks.'

'Anne. Don't worry about an accent. You always kept the accent you had when you left for Australia. Leave it to Dempsey to muddle through what he says to the journalist. Either way, you are his daughter, after all. We don't know much about you ourselves, other than that you are Laura's stepsister.'

'Okay, Mother. I s'pose for a while I should call you Mrs Stanton, if that's all right?'

'Of course it's okay. I'm still hoping that'll be your name one day soon. At least a Mr and Mrs, with Jack. Mightn't be Stanton where you eventually go. But that's fine. Now, c'mon. We've got to get this out of the way, the pair of you.'

Mum looked at us both, then hugged us. She looked older today, more so than the last few days, as we were now into day four of seven. Her hair had got greyer. She wanted this to work just as much as us, so that we could live.

'C'mon Jack,' she said after releasing her hug on us both. 'Get that kettle on again, before they arrive. And Anne—yes you, Laura—no touching Jack, nor Dempsey. And whatever you do, don't shake hands with Will Jacobs, because of the make-up. Plus, no crying either. He's likely to talk about his son's life being saved. Just pretend you are Anne, not Laura. There'll be time for tears once this is over.'

I went to put the kettle on again as the two of them sat on the settee. Once I'd made them tea and joined them in the living room again, there was a knock on the door. It hadn't taken them long. They'd arrived.

As I was standing now in the living room, I went to the front door. Sure enough, as expected, it was Dempsey, and with him was the guy named Will Jacobs.

'Come on in, the pair of you.'

'Thanks, Jack. Good to see you again. Is my other daughter, Anne, here?' Dempsey winked at me so that he couldn't be seen doing so, although he had a serious and stern look on his face.

'She's with Mum, just having a cup of tea, talking about Laura. Come in Will, nice to meet you.' As he came in, I shook his hand, trying to put him at ease.

'Thanks, Jack. You know why I'm here?'

'Well, a couple of reasons, maybe?'

'True. Firstly, could I have a chat with Laura's sister Anne just to clarify the insanity of the story from Mr Dempsey? And secondly, you know what that'll be.'

'Of course you can. Do come on in. I'll make you some tea, kettle's not long boiled. Milk and sugar, Will?'

'Yes, both please. Two sugars.'

'I know you'll have coffee, Dempsey, I'll get you one too.'

'Thank you, Jack.'

We walked into the living room then; Mum and Anne were sitting on the settee.

I introduced Will to Mum and Anne, then went to the kitchen to make their drinks. I could hear their conversation as I made them.

'Hello, Anne. My name's Will Jacobs. Nice to meet you. D'you mind if I ask you a couple of questions please? Your father told me an outrageous story last night.'

'No, that's fine. Nice to meet you. Dad's having a real tough time at present. We all are.'

'I understand. Real sorry for your loss, Anne. But could I just ask you if you've got a picture of your sister, Laura?'

'Well, I do, but not a recent one. I imagine Jack has one, don't you, Jack?'

I'd quickly made the drinks and returned to the living room. 'Yes. I do. Would you like to see it, Will?'

'Please, if it's no trouble. I'm sorry about this, but a journalist's nose is, well, nosy to say the least!'

Putting my drink on the table, I reached into my pocket, taking out my wallet. I always kept a picture of Laura in there. Looking at it myself, then glancing at Anne, I thought Mum had done a good job of changing Laura's appearance. So, I handed over the picture to Will so he could compare it with Anne sitting on the settee.

'Doesn't look much like you, Anne. You've obviously got a tan from Australia. And are you older than Laura?'

I saw Dempsey nod towards her; he must've told Will that she was older.

'Yes, I'm older than Laura.'

'There's eight years difference between them, Will. I'd been married before I met Laura's mother, like I told you earlier,' said Dempsey. There was a pause for a couple of seconds before he continued, as Will inspected the photo, then looked at Anne/Laura, comparing her with the photo. 'Anne's mother remarried after we divorced and they went to Australia, with her new husband. We lost touch over the years, until Laura intervened herself via the internet, finding Anne,' said Dempsey.

It was true he'd been married before, so there was an element of truth to the story.

'Oh, I see. Well, thanks Mr Dempsey. Are you staying long here in town, Anne?'

'No, I'm not, sadly. Laura had invited me to the wedding, but this is so awful. I'm going to spend some time here with Dad and Mrs Stanton, before going back in a few days' time.'

'Thanks, Anne. Sorry to even be asking this, but Mr Dempsey led me to believe that Laura had been re-born.'

'I'd heard Dad likes a drink now and then, spinning the odd yarn?' She looked down at the ground then, avoiding Will's eyes. Her voice was quavering too. I knew she was getting upset.

'All the same, please accept my apologies. But can I say something to you, and to you also, Jack?'

'Fire away, Will, we've got nothing to hide,' I said.

There was a moment of silence then. Will seemed to be getting his composure before speaking.

'Jack, Anne, Mr Dempsey, Mrs Stanton. I'd just like to say...' he paused then, his voice croaking with emotion. I could see his eyes moistening too. 'I can never thank you enough for what Laura did for my wife and myself. Little Tommy was the cause of Laura's demise. I know he never meant it, but I just wanted to have the opportunity to say this to you—and this chance meeting with Mr Dempsey has given me that opportunity—to say thank you for what Laura did. I, for one, shall never, ever, forget what she did for our family.'

I could see tears coming from Will's eyes then, after he had spoken.

We were all quiet then for a few seconds, before Anne/Laura replied. 'That's a wonderful thing to say. I'm sure that she would be so, so pleased to hear that, Will. That gives me and Dad a great deal of comfort right now. Would you excuse me, I need to go to the bathroom. Will, it's been nice to meet you. Keep your family—especially your son Tommy—safe and well, and enjoy a good life.' Her voice was croaky as she stuttered with emotion throughout saying this to Will.

Nobody said another word then as she rose from the settee and walked out of the living room to go upstairs, nodding, then briefly hugging Will, as she did. We all knew what this had meant to her. We knew it was Laura who'd spoken those words. And it looked like tears were about to roll down her cheeks from her already moist eyes as she released him from her arms, turning to look at me. It was too much for her. It was getting too much for all of us. She went directly upstairs then, leaving us with Will in the living room.

You could've heard a pin drop, as there was silence for a few seconds.

'Will, thank you for coming to my cottage. It's been nice to put the silly drunken story to bed. And those words about Laura meant everything to all of us. Thank you, again,' said Mum, replying with tears in her eyes.

'Well, thanks again. I hope you can all get through this. And thank you for what your daughter did, Mr Dempsey.'

'Thanks, Will. I'll see you out,' Dempsey said, in a quivering voice.

Will shook my hand. We didn't speak, just nodded to each other. The silence in the living room again, spoke for all of us as he was leaving. He was going to be eternally grateful for what Laura did that day, saving his son Tommy.

Dempsey walked him to the front door. When the door closed behind Will, Dempsey returned to the room, walking straight up to Mum. I could see he was genuinely upset himself, as his face was red, his eyes moist behind his glasses.

'Mary, I'm so sorry for what I said to you the other night. It was unforgiveable. I wasn't aware of the implications you'd taken on and accepted. I want you to know that anything you want or need help with, you only ever have to ask me. Jack has explained your sacrifice. You know I didn't initially agree with this, but I can never—if this finally works out—truly thank you enough.'

'Dempsey. You old fool, you! You're a good man, we all know that to be true. Just enjoy the time we've all got now. Nobody knows when it'll end. This was a sacrifice worth giving for Jack, and especially Laura. And now, thanks to your concocted stories, we've managed to keep a lid on it for the moment. But no more talking to anyone else about this—especially journalists!'

'Understood loud and clear, Mary.'

The three of us smiled as one. Just then, Laura walked back into the living room from upstairs. We could see streaks down her cheeks where the tanned make-up had run. She'd been to the toilet, but obviously hadn't seen her face in the mirror at all.

We turned our smiles into light laughter when we all saw Laura's face.

'What is it? Jack, Dad, Mother? What is it? I heard the door close. I take it Will's gone now? Hope he's satisfied with the story about my sister Anne. What's so funny?'

I put my arm around her, turning her towards the mirror in the living room. 'Look. Look at you, Anne! Oh! I mean, Laura.'

She joined in our laughter as she saw the messy, streaky lines on her face. Thank God she was out of sight of Will, who'd left a minute or so earlier.

Laura must've read my mind before she spoke. 'Thank goodness he's gone. He'd have had his story, wouldn't he, if I'd come down stairs a couple of minutes earlier!'

'You're not wrong there, daughter. Which daughter are you anyway? Anne or Laura. Oh sorry, I've only got the one daughter.' Said Dempsey, still laughing.

We all continued laughing for a few seconds, until eventually we stopped and Laura spoke seriously.

'Listen. We're safe with me staying in the cottage for now. No point in going outside, not until Harry calls and returns, hopefully by tomorrow. Now, that was a lucky escape. No more incidents like this please, Dad. We've got to keep ourselves to ourselves for a few more days until this is over. There's a lot happening. Mother, you'll have lots of questions to answer. We'll have to work on that too. Let's sort ourselves out now, have a meal in a while, relax, and wait to see if Harry calls. So, nobody talk to any more journalists!'

14. Strength and weakness.

Day four was about to turn into day five after we'd had an early evening meal and Dempsey had gone home shortly afterwards. There had been no call from Harry yet. Laura seemed to be getting stronger and back to her old efficient self, but Mum had been sleeping lots more than usual, I noticed.

Dempsey said he'd keep himself to himself for a few more days until we knew what we had to do.

As Laura was staying out of sight at the cottage, the only person who knew about her fictitious sister Anne was the journalist. We decided that I'd stay there too, as I wanted us to be together.

Mum made contact with Richard Leonard, asking him to keep in touch with her or Dempsey regarding the purchase of the shop. I started to become concerned about Mum, as she seemed to be slowing down in her movements. She'd said it would happen quickly.

I decided to go to the shop, knowing that Dempsey would be there, having said he'd open up for us, seeing as his shop in Hastings had been closed for almost a week now.

Driving to the shop in the morning, I left Mum in bed, with Laura pottering about, tidying up the cottage.

When I arrived, it was good to see that it was open. Dempsey was on his mobile phone when I walked in. The shop was empty. So I went into the back office and put the computer system on, as I'd not logged on for several days, knowing that we'd missed some orders because of Laura's demise.

What I saw amazed me. There were lots of emails from customers, clients, and friends, all saying how sorry they were to hear about Laura's tragic accident. It felt heart-warming to me. Strangely, I looked forward to telling Laura about this when I returned to the cottage later on.

Checking through the emails for a couple of hours, I saw some orders needed processing. So I set about sorting them out as I waited for Harry to call with some news, or better still, when he'd be returning.

Whilst I was doing this, Dempsey came into the back office.

'Hey Jack, good to see you here. Just been on the phone to Richard Leonard. He spoke to your mum at the, er, funeral. He's going to buy, the price is not an issue. Anything he can do to help, he will. And furthermore, he knows from his own experience that this is a great shop and area for antiques, especially with the internet set up you've got.'

'That's great news, thanks. I'll let Laura and Mum know when I go back to the cottage shortly. Just sorting out some orders we've missed,' I replied, pointing at the computer screen.

'Yep, no problem. You carry on, don't worry about the shop. Leave it to me. I'll sort out a deal with Richard. You've a more important issue to be dealing with.'

He was serious. His mood was brighter, almost happy. It was now almost midday on day five, and I'd not heard from Harry. No call at all about any developments. It was getting hard to remain under control, knowing what could happen in a couple of days. I didn't want to lose Laura again.

'Yep. I'll finish up here with these orders, get them posted, then get out of here.'

Which is exactly what I did. The post office was up the road, so I popped there to post half a dozen parcels I'd made up, to go all over the world through the internet site set up by Laura. I'd no idea how Dempsey and Richard would carry on using this system and service, as they were both a bit archaic with their computer skills, if everything went according to our plan.

After visiting the post office, I went back to the cottage. Laura was sitting listening to the radio. We both loved our music, and we always had the radio on in the shop, or wherever we were.

'Hey baby, how'd it go at the shop? Wish I could've gone. Was Dad there?'

'Sent some orders off. Lots of emails all about you, really nice messages too. And yes, your dad was there. Quiet day. Nobody in when I arrived, other than him, on the phone to Richard.'

'Sounds good. Nice about the messages, but a bit surreal, don't you think? Can't wait to get back into it all, I feel more energised each day, y'know. I really don't mind where we go Jack, as long as we're together.'

'Same here. Oh. Nearly forgot. When I said your dad was on the phone to Richard, he told me that he'd buy the shop, take the whole thing over completely. Only thing is, I don't know how, between them, they'll get the hang of the computer system you devised. Can't really give Richard training, especially as you're, er, not here.'

'Good news then. Brilliant! Thought of that already. Been doing a lot of thinking the last couple of days.'

'Intriguing. Tell me more, please,' I said, and I saw her eyes widen, itching to tell me her plan.

'Well, it was strange Harry mentioned New York. I reckon we'll have to go there either way. So why not set up shop there? We can run and control the internet site from there. Name change isn't a problem these days. That can be arranged. Plus, stock can be sent from a hub anywhere nowadays. We can let them both know that we'll have the stock catalogue list wherever we move to, and they can have a stock list, too. From that, we can place orders for them when contacted on the internet. That means they don't have to worry about logging on, keeping stock records, or ordering items and finding them all around the globe. You—and me—can organise that from anywhere in the world. But, the one thing we need, as I've said, is a hub. A base from where stock is posted out. All they'll have to do is record what they've sent, where, when, and who to. We'll just need to email them with what to send where. Most of the time, we'll be giving them all of that information anyway, so they'll end up running the shop—or Richard will—like they've always done, but be post and packaging delivery men, too.'

'Crikey, you've really thought this through, haven't you?'

'Like I said, I've had time to think, and each day I seem to be more energised than before, Jack.'

'Hmm. You being more energetic and Mum being more and more lethargic. You thinking what I'm thinking, Laura?'

'Yes, I am.'

'D'you think that Mum's tiredness equates to you being more energetic and more like your old efficient self—even more so?'

'Possibly and probably, yes.' She paused before continuing. 'I wonder if when Harry gets back—and he'll be back today—whether he'll have the answers for us? I think he will.'

'Well, he hoped he'd be two days, maximum. We need to know about the fourth stone fragment. Its exact whereabouts and location. And what we've got to do with it when we find it.'

'I know. So, in the meantime, I think whilst we're waiting for him to return, you'd better get on to the airport to arrange flights. Doesn't matter when, as long as it's in the next three days. I've been on the internet already in the last couple of days and this morning, while you were at the shop. I've got prices. There are not many flights that give us time to get there. The first thing is to get there. Then we'll worry about the stone afterwards,' she said.

'Great. I'll get on to it now, while we're waiting to hear from Harry. You checked on Mum since I left this morning?'

'She's really tired. I think this is taking its toll on her big time now. Like you said, I'm more energetic, though I still look pale without that make-up on. While I'm getting better, she's getting worse. It doesn't seem fair. I hope she'll be okay when it stops.'

'I know, but there's nothing we can do about that now. Mum did what she did for us. For you. For all of us. So we've got to get on with things.'

Just as I finished saying that, we heard a creak on the stairs. Then Mum walked into the living room.

'How're you two holding up? Seems like the tiredness has kicked in with me already. How'd I look, Laura?'

Laura didn't answer as Mum looked to the mirror in the living room, then turned towards us both and continued talking. 'Now listen, you two. What I did, I did for you both. My hearing's still okay, y'know. I overheard what you said about strength and weakness as I came down the stairs just now. I don't mind this happening, I'd expected it, y'know that. I'll get used to it when it stops. I discussed it with Harry briefly, and he explained it to me from his readings. So life is beginning again, Laura. I've had a good life so far, and I will still have a few more years, God willing. I'll just get older a lot quicker. That's all.'

Laura got up from the settee she was sitting on and hugged Mum. Neither of them said anything else as they held each other. There was nothing more to say. Mum had given part of her life for Laura to return, and was starting to pay the price for that amazing sacrifice.

There were no tears this time, and they eventually let each other go.

'So, you know you're getting stronger, Laura, and I think wiser, too?'

'Yes, I am. I can feel my body being more energised. That's from you, isn't it?'

'It is. And some of my instincts, knowledge and energy may have been passed to you. But it's not possible to know how much, or for how long it'll continue. Harry couldn't find an explanation—not yet anyway—in the book, other than it would happen. Maybe when he returns, he'll know.'

'He'll be back today. I know he will.'

'You said that when I came in from the shop, earlier. Might be that you're getting Mum's insight already, or whatever it is that she's always had. Did you think he'd be back today, Mum?'

'Yes, I did. But the feeling wasn't as strong as before. That's okay, I know Laura will be able to use what she has wisely.'

'I will, Mother. I will.'

'Time for tea, I think, while we wait for Harry to return. I'm not too weak to get that kettle on again,' Mum said, smiling at us both.

When she walked to the kitchen, I looked at Laura, before she spoke.

'I know. Mother looks much older already. But believe it when she says it's what she wants. Remember, she's a remarkable woman, and I know she'll be around for quite a while yet. I know it because I can feel it inside, thanks to her.'

We embraced and kissed, standing in the living room whilst Mum was in the kitchen. Knowing that we'd done the right thing—however amazing—was a comfort to me.

'I love you, Jack. Always have, always will.'

'And I'm in love with you too.'

We stared into each other's eyes, our lips parted for a few seconds as Laura stroked my face. It was so good to be able to hold her again. I hoped that we'd be able to have our wonderful life together, just like we had planned. But it would not be here.

'So, you've got to get on to the airport to arrange the flight, Jack. Time's running out and I want to be with you, to continue our wonderful life.'

'Hey, can you read my thoughts?'

'No, that's something I can't do. Not exactly, anyway. Why?'

'Well, I was thinking exactly what you just said.'

'Really? Maybe when we're close I can, or it could just be coincidence. One thing's for sure Jack, it'll keep you on your toes, won't it?'

'Too right it will!'

Then we smiled again as she let her hand fall from my face.

'Now, airport booking, please,' said Laura, before continuing. 'You know Harry said he thinks the stone may be in New York, so let's hope he's right. We've a flight to arrange. You sort that out and I'll help in the kitchen. I'm getting back, more and more, to my old efficient self!'

'Hmm. Don't I just know it! Okay, I'm on it now.'

'Good.'

Although still pale, Laura was getting stronger as Mum was getting weaker. Nothing I could do about that now. So I set about organising flights for us.

15. Harry's return.

So, I sat with the computer for an hour or so, trawling through flights, before contacting the airport and travel companies. Laura had organised a lot of the ground work with prices already.

'Laura?' I called out to her, as she was in the kitchen with Mum still.

She came into the living room then. 'What is it, baby? Any joy yet?'

'Yep, got us on a flight tomorrow night, that's the first one available. That's the sixth day, so we'll not have a lot of time when we get there.'

'I know. But it'll work out, Jack. I feel it.'

'I'm glad you do, that intuition thing is keeping me calm right now.'

'Don't worry, it really will be okay.'

She put her hands round my neck as I sat on the settee, leaning over me whilst I was getting the details from the computer for the flights. It felt good, with her wrapping her arms around me momentarily.

'Good. Now, all we've got to do is wait for Harry to get back, to let us know where to go when we get there. And it has to be New York now, we've just booked the flights!' I said, breaking our brief silence.

'He'll be in touch soon, Jack.'

As if she knew—and she sort of did—my mobile phone went off, just as I was making a note of the flight details.

I stood up from the settee as it rang. Laura dropped her arms from around my neck. She'd been perched on the corner of the settee at the time.

'It's Harry, isn't it?'

I nodded, slightly open-mouthed. It was.

'Hey, is that you, Harry?'

'Yes, it's me, Jack. D'you want to come and pick me up from the airport? I've literally just landed, and time's going by really quickly, I'm sure you know that already.'

'Yep. I'll jump in the car straight away. You can tell me all about it when I pick you up. You should've called, and I'd have got there when you arrived.'

'Sorry, got a cancellation booking, I'm a few hours earlier than my original flight.'

'Okay. I'll meet you at the same place I dropped you off, d'you remember?'

'No problem. See you in about an hour or so. Drive safely, brother.'

I cut off the phone as Laura stared at me.

Mum came in from the kitchen.

'He's back then?'

'Yes, Mum. Just landed.'

'Get yourself going, then. Drive carefully. No speeding. The weather is bad out there right now. I'll make some dinner for when you're back in a few hours, okay?'

'Will do. Thanks.'

I kissed Mum on the cheek, then kissed Laura, grabbed my keys, and left the cottage in seconds, going straight to the car. It was late afternoon now, with windy and wet weather conditions. I knew the drive and route, having done it a few times before over the years, and thought to myself that I'd have to be cautious on the road.

It took about an hour and a half to get to Harry at the airport, longer than normal. I knew that I'd be doing this journey again with Laura the next day. Harry was waiting at the same place I'd dropped him off at.

'How'd it go, Harry?'

'Let's get in the car first and I'll tell you all about it.'

We embraced quickly and I put his bag in the boot of the car. It was still raining hard. Driving off, I waited for Harry to tell me what he'd managed to find out.

'Is Mum okay? How's she doing? Is she ageing?' he asked.

'She's okay. Ageing more. She's got a lot of grey hair now. She's really tired, though there's nothing wrong with her hearing, as she heard us talking about her earlier!'

'Glad she can hear okay, she always had that,' Harry said, laughing momentarily. 'The ageing is to be expected, but it should settle down by the end of the seven days, I hope. Did she tell you that this'd happen, Jack? She knew before we started this a few days ago. I wasn't sure to what extent and speed it'd get her, though we both knew she'd age twenty-five years. It's was the only way. Like she said, there had to be a sacrifice. Sorry I didn't tell you before it happened. Mum made me promise we wouldn't tell you until afterwards. I know we've always had an honest relationship since we were kids, so I just want to say sorry. She thought that you'd maybe not go through with it at the start, and that we had to convince you it'd work.'

'No, she never said what would happen to her. But that's fine. I understand. But the problem's Laura, even more so than Mum. She's so pale.'

'Yep, I know. When I left a couple of days ago I could see she was. But that should change, with the other fourth stone, I'm hoping.'

'Well, although she's pale, her energy levels are getting back to normal. It seems that Mum's tiredness—and her ageing—is directly opposite to Laura. She's positively buzzing right now.'

'Thought that'd happen, though it'll probably be temporary. Like I said, Mum knew about this before we started and she was prepared to accept the consequences. Once the ageing has finished—and I know I'm repeating myself here—she'll settle down and hopefully get used to her new, older body.'

'Mind you, there's another side effect I've noticed in the last couple of days, while you've been in Ireland.'

'What's that?'

'Hmm, well you know Mum's always had this sort of intuition, knowing when we'd call her and things like that?'

'Yep, she always seemed to know where we were and what we were up to.'

'Seems that some of that has passed onto Laura.'

'Wow! Didn't expect that to happen. Mind you, it's possibly, just a temporary thing. Not sure how long that'll last either.'

'Got to keep an eye on both of them still. Now, what've you found out at the seminary from those elders, and that original Book of Scrolls?'

Harry grabbed a bottle of water out of his pocket, took a swig and then started to talk again. 'Right. I've been with the elders—two of them in fact—who are literally the oldest priests at the seminary. With their help, I've managed to translate bits of the book I couldn't before. It's not written that the fourth stone is in New York, as that happened more recently. Fortunately, we know where it is, so you've both got to go there, Jack. No choice, though you knew that anyway.'

'I've sorted out flights for me and Laura already, but it's cutting it fine. I couldn't get a flight until tomorrow, Saturday. It's the sixth day of the seven.'

'You've got a flight though, Jack. That's the most important thing. So, we know where the fourth stone is, and you can get there. Not much time, but that's fine. It's at the museum, and your big problem is getting inside. One of the elders told me that once the incantations have been said, there's no need to say them again. What you've to do is get Laura inside to actually hold the stone. She doesn't need to say anything.'

'And will that bring her back, Harry?'

'Well, you know when Mum used the three stones at the shrine, behind the chapel?'

'Yep, course I do.'

'They were all touching Laura. That's why she has to physically touch the fourth stone. The elders told me she's only here temporarily because we only had three stones, not all four of them like I'd presumed. The elders didn't know how long she'd survive with one stone missing. But I knew from what I'd translated that it was only the seven days we're in right now. So, we're all right until midnight on day seven. You have to get her into the museum, Jack. To hold that stone.'

'And that's it. She'll return for good. Forever?'

'Technically yes, that's right.'

'But there's something else, Harry, isn't there?'

'Hmm. I had an idea that she'd have to hold the stone, but I had to check with the elders. The story is so obscure and slightly vague, as it's been verbally passed down over the years from elder priest to elder priest. There is something else, but neither of them, nor The Book of Scrolls once I'd translated it, could tell me what. There's a section at the bottom of a page in the book that's so old it's withered away and is unreadable. Jack, I'm sorry, but I don't know what it is, the words are almost illegible. I've taken copies of the page on my phone to keep working on it, as there are some letters I can read, and some I can't. But it's guess work as to what it means. I'll keep on trying for you, you know that.'

'So, even getting there to the museum, finding the stone, and getting Laura to it, still might not be enough?'

'Jack, I know it might feel like falling at the final hurdle, but you've got to keep your faith and believe.'

'I do. I will. It's just so tough to know that it mightn't actually work after all everyone's been through. And to lose her now, when she's really back.'

We stopped talking then. As I'd driven home, we'd got caught in traffic. The rain was still teeming down, although the high winds had eased. Sitting silently for a while, I put the radio back on, and Harry began dozing off.

After another hour, we'd got back home.

'Thanks Jack, for picking me up,' Harry said, stirring from his slumber.

'Hey, for what you've been doing for us, I'd go to the ends of the earth for you, brother. You know that, don't you?'

'Sure. Sure I do.' He smiled at me then, as we both got out of the car simultaneously.

'Come on, you'll have to repeat that all again to Laura and Mum.'

'I will, but don't mention the page to Laura that's unreadable. I'll keep working on it. Don't want to worry her unduly. She may lose faith herself.'

'Harry, I've got no secrets from her. Remember you said that you'd wanted to tell me about Mum's ageing? Well, we've got to tell Laura. She'll understand, Harry. And the way her intuition is, I know she's likely to know something's up.'

'Okay. We'll tell them everything. Even about that page in the book.'

'Good. C'mon, let's get in out of the rain.'

We'd been standing talking behind the back of the car, getting Harry's bag out and we were both now pretty wet, so I grabbed the bag and we went into the cottage.

'Hey, Mum. How're you feeling?'

'I'm tired, Harry. But well. Was it a productive journey? Did Jack tell you about the flights?'

'He did, yes. Now, let me get my coat off and I'll tell you both all about what's going on. How are you, Laura?'

'Apart from being very pale, Harry, I'm feeling really good. I'm sure Jack's told you about me being more energetic. It's a side effect of what's been going on between me and your mother.'

'I know. That's partly to be expected, though Jack said you've been getting feelings of intuition like Mum always does. I don't know if that's likely to stay with you. Not sure about that. You'll have to wait and see how that develops.'

'Right, I'll put the kettle on. Harry, you tell Mum and Laura what you told me in the car. Everything. And what we've got to do next.' I put my arm around Laura and kissed her before going to make tea.

'Will do. Now listen you two, here's where we are.'

I went into the kitchen, but could hear Harry talking. He repeated all that he'd told me in the car as I waited for the kettle to boil, about the two elders and the story being passed down from priest to priest, the fourth stone being needed to be held by Laura. And finally he told them about the missing information on that vital page from the Book of Scrolls.

The tea was made, so I took it back into the living room. Mum and Laura were sitting on the settee, and Harry was in the armchair. He looked tired. I'm sure he was.

'So, where do we go from here, Harry?' I said.

'We've to figure out a way of getting you both into that museum, to that fourth stone.'

'I've been checking the internet already, while you were on the way back from the airport,' said Laura. 'The museum is open seven days a week. Luckily, we'll be there on Sunday, all being well. It's only open from ten a.m. until five thirty p.m., so we'll have to get cracking once we get off the plane. There's a display on the first floor, of ancient artefacts and stones. And I've seen a picture of the stone fragment. Your Mother's shown me the other three stones again. They definitely match up as one. I think I know exactly where it is on the first floor. Trouble is, it's in a sealed glass cabinet. I can't tell from the internet whether it's safety glass or not. So, when we get there, I've got a plan to get it out of the glass cabinet.'

'Crikey, you are on the ball!' I said, raising my eyebrows at her ingenuity.

'You know me well, Jack. I try not to leave any stone unturned.'

We all began to laugh when she said this. But not for long. She didn't laugh, just smiled at us all, before carrying on with her idea.

'Right, now, I've taken photos of the three stones here, you'll need to get them printed off at the shop, Jack. I'll take them in my suitcase, along with some clothes, of course. When we get to the museum, I'm going to ask to be shown the stone. I've sent an email in advance to let the curator know that I've got access to the other three fragments, which make up the whole stone, asking if I—we—can try and match up the photos with their stone.'

'Sounds like a plan to me,' I said.

'It is, Jack. And I know it'll work too. I've only to hold the stone in my hand, and then this'll be over, I hope. We hope. But, the only thing is, this page Harry can't read, means there's maybe more to it than simply holding it. Let's just get over there. I've got faith in you, Harry. We all have.'

'Thanks. I'll work on trying to decipher what it says, but there are only a few letters legible.'

'No matter. Right now, I think you need to rest, Harry. Have the cuppa Jack made, then let's eat. Then, as Mother's getting tired again and it's getting late, we'd better all hit the sack. We can start afresh tomorrow, before we leave for the airport. Sounds like a plan, don't you agree?' said Laura, smiling at all of us.

'Well, I'm impressed. I've always said you're efficient!'

'You know me, baby. So, so well. C'mon, drink your tea all of you I'll go and cook something up in the kitchen.'

'I'll give you a hand, Laura.'

'No, that's fine, Mother. You take it easy. Please. I'm sure Jack can give me a hand, anyway.'

'Yep, you two take it easy. Harry, you have a rest, seriously. You've had a long few days.'

'Thanks, Jack.'

'Right, to the kitchen,' Laura said, looking at me.

As I walked into the kitchen, a few moments after her, I could see Laura already had tears in her eyes. She put her finger to her mouth so that I was quiet.

'What is it?' I whispered to her.

'Jack, I'm worried. About everything. Mother ageing. Harry mightn't be able to find out what's missing in that page, and we really don't know what we've—or I've—got to do when we get the stone, or if we've enough time when we get there. And we don't even know if they'll let us take it out of the cabinet at the museum.'

She was sobbing now, quietly.

I looked her in the eyes, kissing her gently on the lips. 'Don't worry. It'll all come out in the wash.'

She smiled then. It was a silly catch phrase that Mum always used to use when we were going out together. She never worried about anything herself, and I knew that I was just like her in many ways.

'You know I'm right, don't you?' I continued.

'Yes. I do. Sorry. It's just that I don't want to lose you again.'

'Now listen, Laura Dempsey. Don't be sorry. That's not happening. Remember, keep the faith. I don't want to lose you either. We'll prevail. We've come a long way already. It will all be good. I promise.'

'Okay. Thanks.'

We cuddled each other then, but I thought Laura looked paler than when I'd left to drive to the airport. It concerned me, but I said nothing to her. And I was getting worried myself that Harry wouldn't be able to find out what had been written on that page in the book. I knew it was important, especially from his reaction when he'd said initially to say nothing about it to Mum and Laura. But I kept those thoughts to myself. I had to stay positive and keep believing, too. Harry returned, and he'd got some more information. We were a little bit closer to bringing Laura back for good.

'Now, I think you'd better call your Dad to keep him in the loop about everything, don't you?' I asked Laura.

'S'pose I should really. Just hope he doesn't go off on one about it. He's said he's stopped drinking now until this is all over, especially after that slip up with Will Jacobs.'

'He's got a right to know. It's only fair,' I said. 'Without him, you'd not have had the chance to be here. You know that.'

'I know, you're right Jack. I'll call him now.'

She did call him, on the upstairs phone. When she'd finished, she came back into the kitchen. Harry and Mum were sitting, resting quietly in the living room, and she walked past them into the kitchen.

'He's not happy about us not knowing exactly what we've to do, Jack.'

'Well, we've got no choice but to carry on. We'll do this.'

'Yes, we will.'

I reached out and held her in my arms again for a few moments, standing silently, knowing how hard this all must be for her. She was the one who might disappear, so I knew I had to stay strong and focused for myself, but more importantly, for Laura. Eventually, she broke the silence.

'Right, you, let's cook a nice meal for Mother, and for Harry's return.'

'Yep. I know just what to do. Mum's old recipe. And you know, it's my favourite, and Harry's.'

'Think I know what that is.'

'Yes, you do. And Harry's not had it since his last visit months ago. Mum always makes it for him. So now it's our turn.'

'Great. Meat and potato pie it is then, Jack.'

'Spot on. The right meal for Harry's return.'

So we got the ingredients and made our favourite meal. The good old meat and potato pie. Especially for me and Harry, of course.

16. Cracking the code.

About an hour or so later, the meat and potato pie was ready. We all sat down for the meal. Harry was tired, just like Mum had become. We were all quiet eating our meal, as it was late in the evening.

Once we'd finished, Harry came into the kitchen with me to help with the washing up, leaving Laura and Mum at the table.

'It'll all work out, Jack.'

'You know what, I think it will,' I said, trying to exude confidence in my voice.

We said no more to each other, just quietly got on with washing up the plates, pots, and pans. Just like we always used to when we were kids.

'Right, that's all sorted. Just like the old days, eh, Jack?'

'Yep, just like old times.'

'I'm having a cuppa, then its bed for me soon. You want one?'

'Not for me, thanks,' I replied.

'A clear head tomorrow, after a good kip is what I need.'

'Okay, Harry, you've had a long couple of days. I'd imagine you're dog tired now.'

'Yep. The flights—although not long—catch up with you.'

'Mum's left the old camp bed in the parlour for you. You're privileged, remember when we were never allowed in there when she used to do all her readings?'

'Hmm. I sure do. That'll be nice again. Hope she's put her vases and bits away so I don't knock them over!' he said, laughing.

'Think she'd have done that ages ago. We both used to be clumsy back then. I'm still a bit like that even now!' I replied, smiling.

'Well, I've grown out of that, Jack, somewhat, fortunately.'

'Good to hear it. Well, I'm still clumsy. Always was more so than you, wasn't I?'

'You were. But no place like home. Mind you, if this all works out, you'll have a new home, somewhere else.'

'I know, it'll be strange. But it doesn't matter where we are. We'll be together. That's all that matters, y'know.'

'That's all there is to it, Jack. You've got the faith to believe it. Now, I'm going to say goodnight to those two ladies in there. I need to get to bed shortly,' said Harry.

'Okay.'

We hugged each other, saying nothing else.

He walked into the living room with his cuppa, whilst I finished off tidying the kitchen, listening to their conversation.

'Mum, I'm off to bed. Jack's said the camp bed's ready for me in the parlour. Thanks.'

'Oh yes. Forgot to mention that earlier, son.'

'Fine, Mum. I'll be careful.'

'Everything's in boxes now. I packed most of it away a while ago. Felt the need to do so.'

'Got a lot of "stuff" in there, Mum.'

'I know. It's all for you, Jack, and Laura. Not right now, but it's for all of you. Y'know?'

'I know, Mum. Thanks.'

As I came in from the kitchen, I saw Harry bend down and kissed Mum, hugging her as she sat on the settee. Then he leant towards Laura, hugging her too, kissing her on the cheek.

'Good night, Laura. Sleep well when you eventually go to bed. I'll see you all in the morning, when I shall try and crack the code of the book.'

'Night, Harry,' I said, coming into the living room.

'Goodnight, Jack.'

Then he sauntered off to bed, taking his tea with him. It was getting late, almost eleven o'clock, at the end of day five. We needed Harry's expertise tomorrow to try and find the missing letters or words to help us. Nothing we could do now but all get to bed ourselves, I thought.

'You off to bed as well, Mum?'

'Yes, I'm tired too.'

'Okay. Get yourself up those apples and pears!' I said light heartedly.

'Will do, young fella,' she replied, smiling. 'Night Laura. See you in the morning.'

She kissed me, then Laura, and went out of the living room, up to her bedroom.

Laura and I were left alone in the living room. We'd not had much time alone at all yet, what with everything that had been happening since her return.

'You want to go to bed too?'

'Yes please, Jack.'

'You're keen?'

'Absolutely. I feel the need to make love to you, Jack,' she said quietly.

She was never slow in coming forward. That's why I loved her so much. And we'd not made love at all since she'd returned, with her initial tiredness having intervened.

I took her hand and stood in front of her whilst she sat on the settee. We said nothing else. As she stood up, I could see her pale complexion was still the same, and I kissed her as she got to her feet. But as I touched her face, I could feel the softness of her skin, which I loved.

Walking out of the living room, up the stairs, we still said nothing to each other. We didn't need to. We'd always been comfortable with each other anywhere, whether we were talking, or not.

Reaching the spare bedroom—mine and Harry's old room—we only had a single bed to squeeze into together. But no matter, we made the most of what we had. No way could we go to the flat; she'd be seen. But as long as we were together, it really didn't matter where we were.

Her strength and energy was getting better every day, she was always alert, I thought, especially mentally, more so than before, it seemed.

Oh, how I loved her body. It was pale, almost transparent, but I closed my eyes when we got into bed, touching her all over, just feeling her skin under my hands. She was, to me, truly beautiful.

We began to make love slowly and quietly, not wanting to disturb Mum. We giggled a couple of times and Laura whispered that she felt like a naughty school girl. It did feel like that, even for me, too. It was wonderful to be so close to her once again, as we gently continued to make love to each other...

Holding each other close, we eventually fell asleep wrapped up in each other's arms. I slept soundly, knowing for the next couple of days, she was with me. But I hoped it would be for good, with Harry's help trying to crack the code.

***

The next morning, as I awoke, Laura was already up and out of bed. I could hear the shower going in the bathroom. So, I got out of bed, put my old dressing gown on, and went into the bathroom, knowing it would be her in there. I could hear her singing. It was our song, 'Our Day Will Come'. Even with her atrocious voice, I could tell that was what she was singing!

'Hey, nice singing.' I lied. 'I recognise that song.'

'Oh! Morning, baby. Sleep well?'

Yes, I did actually.'

'Me too. Thanks to you,' she said, smiling at me.

'Hmm, very nice,' I said, as I peeked around the shower curtain to see her lovely naked body. Still pale, but lovely, I thought.

'Cheeky!'

'You fancy a cuppa? I'll go and put the kettle on for us.'

'Yes please, Jack. I'll be down shortly when I'm dressed, then you can have a shower after me. Oh, and just one other thing.' There was a few seconds silence, before she stared into my eyes and said, 'I love you.'

'And I love you too,' I replied, as I leant towards her for a kiss, both of us smiling afterwards. Then I left, going downstairs to make us some tea.

Harry was already there.

'Tea?' he asked me.

'Yep, thanks. One for me and one for Laura, too.'

'On the way. No sugar still for either of you?'

'Nope. As Mum used to say to us, sweet enough, eh, brother?'

'Yep, apparently so,' he said, laughing.

'I'll make you some breakfast if you want some, Harry?'

'That'd be nice, thanks. Then I'll get on with the book, have a look at that today. I feel more refreshed after a good night's sleep. I slept really well in the parlour, forgotten how comfy that old camp bed was.'

'Good. What d'you fancy, toast, cereal?'

'A couple of slices of toast, please.'

'Think I'll join you.'

'Get the engine started with something light in the morning. I usually have some toast after early morning prayers at the seminary, actually.'

Harry rarely spoke about his time there, other than that he prayed and preached a lot. For him to say something about it was unusual.

'And what does the rest of a normal day consist of, Harry?'

'Well, early morning prayers. Breakfast. Reading time until early afternoon. Each day is different. Mass either in the morning or evening, and then I help out in the kitchen for an evening meal with the cooks. Quite enjoy that.'

'Sounds like it's a busy life being a priest.'

'Can be. Especially when you get involved with the community. But I'm here now, and I've got a job to do for you. Now, where's my toast?'

I knew when Harry had finished what he wanted to say because he'd either change the subject or ask a question himself. And he'd just said more than he'd ever said before about his time in the seminary as I prepared the toast for him.

'Here you go.'

'Thanks.'

I put some more bread in the toaster for myself. Just after it'd popped up, Laura came into the kitchen.

'Toast. For me? Thanks,' she said, taking the plate with two slices of toast straight out of my hand, laughing at me as she did so.

What could I do? I put some more bread in for me.

When my toast was ready, I went and joined the two of them at the table in the kitchen.

'Enjoy the toast, did you?'

'Sorry, Jack. I know it's cheeky of me, but you know me well. And you love me.'

'Yes, it was cheeky and I don't mind. And yes, I love you,' I replied, smiling at her, not feeling at all embarrassed in front of my brother.

We all sat eating breakfast for a few minutes before Harry spoke again.

'Okay then, I'm going to get these photos on my phone printed out, so that I can try and decipher some of these words, or at least a few of the letters.   Where's the printer Jack, you've got one I take it?'

'Yep, but it's at the shop. I'll take you there once we've eaten breakfast. Didn't think about that last night, Harry.'

'Not to worry, shouldn't take too long. You've got your computer there to plug into?'

'Yep, got all the mod cons of the computer world there.'

'Good. If you don't mind, I'll grab a shower first, then we'll go.'

'I need a quick shower too, Harry, so I'll go up now. Finish my toast when I get back down, save time. I'll look in on Mum while I'm up there.'

'Right.'

So I left some of my toast, had a sip of my tea, and went up for a quick shower. It was almost nine o'clock now on day six, so we needed to get a move on.

Once we'd both showered and got dressed, it was nearly ten o'clock, so we left the cottage after I'd checked on Mum, who was still sleeping.

Getting to the shop, Dempsey was there, having just opened up. We said good morning, going directly to the office behind the main shop.

Harry took out his mobile phone, for which he had a lead to plug into the computer. We saw the images of the photos on the screen, which I couldn't read nor understand, as they were in an ancient Gaelic dialect. Harry was staring at them, trying to see if he could make them out or not.

'You want print outs then, Harry?'

'Yes. As big as possible. That okay?'

'Course it is. Not a problem. Just give me about twenty minutes, I'll have to switch on the printer first and get some more paper.'

'I'll have a wander around the shop then, if it's all right, Jack?'

'Absolutely. Have a chat with Dempsey, see what his mood's like.'

'Okay.'

Harry went into the main shop, leaving me to fix up the printer with paper and get several different sized photos printed for us—but mainly for him—to have a look at. I could overhear his conversation with Dempsey clearly while I set up the printer.

'Morning again, Mr Dempsey. Quiet day in the shop so far?'

'I'll shut the shop, Harry. Call me Dempsey, everybody does.'

I heard the click of the lock of the front door before either of them spoke again.

'Harry, it's good to see you, but the circumstances are not the best, are they?'

'Well, you know as much as the rest of us, and what needs to be done. Jack told me your feelings about all this, that it's wrong to tamper with good and evil. But you know that this has had implications for our Mum as well. She's prepared to sacrifice, and has done so, a part of her life for Laura.'

'I know that Harry, but if Laura doesn't get to that fourth stone, it's all over. Mary would've aged needlessly and Laura could end up roaming the earth as a lost soul. You've got to see where I'm coming from. I know it sounds awful for me to say, but I'd rather this never happened, especially as you still don't know if they can get to New York in time.'

'Well, flights have been arranged for this evening, for both of them.' I could hear Harry's calm voice, although Dempsey's was getting louder and more vociferous.

'Even so, it's all so, so higgledy-piggledy, all over the place. How can it possibly work? This is like something out of a science fiction story!'

'But it's not though, is it? We are making this happen, all of us. Faith has got us this far. You should hold onto that yourself, Dempsey. I know you've been wavering in your beliefs, but I truly believe this'll work out for the best.'

'I just don't know, Harry. I just don't know!' Dempsey said, with anger still in his tone.

There was silence between the two of them then, and I finished setting up the printer, sorted out some copies, and went into the main shop.

'Right Harry, printer's sorted. You want to have a look at what we've got?'

'Yep, let's go see what there is.'

'What're you looking at, anyway, the pair of you?' said Dempsey, still in an agitated manner.

'It's the copy of The Book of Scrolls page. The one that's sort of not legible, hey, Harry?'

'I can make out some words, but need to have a closer look to try and understand what might be written there,' Harry replied.

'For God's sake you two! This is crazy! Even now, with only a couple of days left, you still don't know what needs to be done!' shouted Dempsey.

'You know we're working on this to keep your daughter alive, don't you, Dempsey?' replied Harry, calmly.

'I know that! But even you don't know what these missing words are. You're just guessing now.'

'Not exactly. I can understand most of the language, but can't see what words and letters are missing. With these print outs of the pages, I'll have a better chance of reading it, so I can try and make out what it says.'

'Like I said, you're not sure what needs to be done still. Ridiculous! Madness! I want no more to do with this. You shouldn't be doing this. I wish I'd never got involved now. Should've left Laura where she was.'

I had returned to lean over the computer when I heard him say that.

'Don't say that, Dempsey! You don't mean that, surely? You know what we'd planned together, we're meant to be together, and we've got a chance here!' I shouted at him.

'Just get out of the shop when you've finished. I'm closing up early. I'll make sure I get you a deal with Richard, but once that's done, I don't want to see you ever again, Jack!'

'You don't mean that, Dempsey,' said Harry. 'You can't blame Jack for all of this. It's not even over yet. Look, we've got a chance to bring Laura back for good.'

'Doesn't matter, Harry. Jack knows I blame him for this. It's like one big, mad, sad fantasy. But it's not. It's happening. Well, I've seen Laura. She's as white as a sheet. Looks like she's fading fast. And now your mother? God, she's ageing so fast, who knows how long she'll live? It's not right. We've broken God's holy law here. I wish I'd never got involved!'

'Too late for that now, Dempsey,' I shouted back at him. 'We've still got time on our side. You wait and see. C'mon, Harry, let's get these sheets back to the cottage where we can study them, see if you can't decipher them before we go to New York.'

'And that's a bloody joke as well! How're you going to get to the stone in that museum anyway?'

'No point me explaining any more to you, Dempsey, not while you're in this frame of mind,' I said, with a more calm and controlled voice now.

'Jack? Harry? It's not right. I'm sorry I ever got involved. You talked me into it. Like I already said, she's going to roam the earth as a spirit or a lost soul. You'd be better off joining her, Jack.'

Harry shouted back at him, 'Dempsey! Don't think that of anyone. Be careful what you wish for, it may be you who suffers the consequences!'

Harry was angry when he spoke, I could see it. I'd hardly ever heard him raise his voice in anger before.

I put my hand on Harry's shoulder, turning him away from this face to face confrontation with Dempsey.

'C'mon, Harry. Let's go. Keep in touch, Dempsey. We've got work to do.'

We left the shop, not saying goodbye to Dempsey at all. He'd burnt his bridges with us all now, I thought. And his own daughter. As we got in the car to go back to the cottage, I could see Harry visibly shaking with rage.

'Harry, it's okay. He blames me for all of this.'

'But he's such a fool. I know we've got to sort out this missing information, but we've still got a chance. Can't he see that?'

'No, obviously not anymore. He's a big believer in the afterlife staying just that. Even with him being involved in bringing Laura back, his own consciousness can't accept it. Maybe he thinks with you being a priest, you're going against God's holy law as well.'

'I get that. But it's written in the ancient Book of Scrolls. We know that. He knows that.'

'Now calm down, Harry. Never thought I'd say that to you. Let's get back so you can have a look at these copies of the page. We're seriously running out of time now.'

'Okay, Jack. You're right. Sorry for raising my voice there.'

We sat silently then as Harry began to study the copies of the page that had been damaged, apart from a few letters and words. With busy traffic, some fifteen minutes later we'd arrived at the cottage. Going straight inside, Harry sat at the living room table. I went and made tea for us whilst he started to study the copies of the page.

'Hey, boys. You've seen Dempsey?'

'Yes, Mum. Not a happy bunny right now. Lost his temper when we went to the shop to get copies of the page from Harry's phone so he could try and understand what it says.'

'I'd partly expected that.'

'Is that perception, Mum, or your intuition?' asked Harry.

'No. Laura said he'd "flip his lid", in her own words.'

'She was right there. Where is she now? Hope she's not gone out, it'll just make things worse if she's seen by anyone who knows her,' I said.

'No, Jack. She's upstairs. Took your laptop computer up there. When you booked the flights, she checked where the museum is in relation to the airport at New York, and it's about forty miles away at the most. She's trying to organise a hire car to save time.'

'I didn't think of that. Just wanted to get flights.'

'That's okay, just before you came in she shouted downstairs to me that she's sorted a car out.'

'Great. Thank goodness for that.'

'Now, let's pop into the kitchen and have that tea. I'll make you both a sandwich if you want one. We can leave Harry here studying these copies of the page in peace and quiet. That okay, Harry?'

'Yep, good idea, Mum,' he replied, not even looking up from the copied pages of the book.

Just then, Laura came downstairs.

'Mother tell you I've sorted out a car when we get there, Jack?'

'Yep, thanks. I just forgot about it.'

'Not a problem.' She kissed me then, and we walked into the kitchen, leaving Harry to study the pages in the living room.

Mum made some sandwiches for all of us, taking one to Harry and returning to us in the kitchen. I'd closed the door to leave Harry alone for about an hour or so, whilst we chatted amongst ourselves.

'Mum, Dempsey lost the plot when we were at the shop. Even Harry raised his voice. I've never seen my brother angry like that.'

'You've got to understand how his mind is working. You may not even know this, Laura, but when you were very young and your own mother passed away, I knew Dempsey then. Your father was a kind, devoted husband. A gentleman.' She stopped talking then to have a bite of a sandwich. 'So, when your mother passed away—God rest her soul—he was distraught, as you can imagine. You were only about three or four years old.'

'I do have pictures and some memories of my mum, but there's never been any on show in our house,' Laura said.

'That's because I spent time with your father after your mother passed away. He came to me for some readings. But after those two or three visits, I never saw him again, other than passing by saying hello. He didn't want any memories of her, only in his head, he told me back then. People grieve in different ways. I knew then your father needed consoling. Comforting. I read his palms. Told him some things that were coming to fruition. That was pretty much one of the last times I saw him, or you, until you came to our cottage when you were both kids, on Jack's sixteenth birthday.'

'What d'you mean, Mum?' I asked.

'Jack. Oh, Jack. I've known that you two would—or could—be together from the day that Dempsey came to see me, after your Mother passed away Laura.'

'How? What did you say to him then?' questioned Laura.

'I told him he'd have a good life, Laura. And that one day in the future when you were older, he'd be needed to help you. It would be important to your life. And, I said that he would have a good business all of his life. But there was something I couldn't tell him, nor will I tell either of you.'

'I understand that, Mum. So, that had to be twenty years ago? And then you never really saw him or spoke to him until that night on my birthday when I was sixteen?'

'Correct, son. That night, almost ten years ago, I reminded him again about what I'd said. But I never mentioned you two. That would be tempting fate. He mayn't have believed me, though I could see on that evening way back then, the look you both had in your eyes.'

Laura and I smiled at each other, before she spoke. 'Why is he so angry then?'

'Well, Laura. When I first told him this, he walked out of this cottage disbelieving what I'd said. He'd heard stories about my reading of cards and palms and wasn't sure about visiting me. The thing is, when I spoke to him to find out about who he was before reading his palms, he told me he was a seventh son of a seventh son.'

'Mum! You're the same as well. Seventh daughter of a seventh daughter.'

'Yes. I knew that then, all those years ago. There was no way I could say anything to Dempsey. He'd literally, a few weeks before, lost your own mother, Laura. He was still distraught. Thing is, I knew what this meant, from my own beliefs and readings. It spurred me on, to investigate the story I'd heard about The Book of Scrolls being able to bring someone back to life. The only place where in-depth knowledge was kept was in Ireland, where we'd come from when you and Harry were young boys, Jack.'

'How'd you know Harry would go there? And that he'd become a priest?'

'That was your brother's own doing. He's always been fascinated by astrology, as you know. Initially, after finishing university, he read up on religious artefacts. So, as you also know, when he was twenty one—straight out of university—he said he wanted to become a priest. Initially, it was to study ancient artefacts and religious symbols. Thing is, he chose Ireland to go to himself, though I suggested the exact seminary he went to, knowing that The Book of Scrolls was there.'

'Harry didn't know about all of this being possible, Mum?'

She picked up one of the plates with another sandwich, taking it into Harry, then returned to the kitchen.

'No, he didn't. Not all of it. It was only when he started to find out about the book from the elders at the seminary that he started to piece things together. When you two met, he never knew about the book, all those years ago.'

'So when did he work out what could happen?' questioned Laura.

'Well, it was when he went to the seminary. He already knew about my mother and myself being seventh born. Before he went, I told him about your father too, Laura. I sowed a seed in his mind, about the possibility of information in the book, knowing his interest in astrology, artefacts, and religious study.'

'You left him to work out what might be written, about what could happen?'

'Sort of, Jack. I knew that Harry could read the Gaelic language. Especially the ancient writings in the book. That's something I couldn't master when I'd seen a copy in the library. But he could. I knew that might—just might—be needed one day. Now, that day has come.'

'Wow! You knew this'd happen, Mum?'

'No. Didn't expect it, but sort of knew of the possibility if it was ever needed. I didn't know everything, but most of it. But, I wasn't aware of what would change me though, until Harry explained it a week ago.'

'Mum. You're amazing.'

I stood up then and hugged her. Laura sat smiling. It was as if she'd known all this, and then she said, 'No, I didn't know all of this Jack, if that's what you're thinking.'

'Well, I sort of was thinking that, actually,' I said, before Laura continued.

'That wasn't mind reading. As well as all of this, she told me that the seminary is in County Tyrone, where you all grew up until coming here years ago. That influenced Harry's decision to go and train there, so he could also check up on your family tree. Mother told me all of this, this morning, while you were at the shop.'

'Oh. Good. Where does it leave us now, though?'

'Relying on your brother,' said Mum. 'Let's leave him a bit longer. He's got something to eat now, and a cuppa. He needs time to try and translate what he can see.'

I sat back down at the kitchen table then. All three of us carried on eating for a few minutes until Laura spoke again. 'Right. We've got flights, a hire car, and we know where the museum is. When we get there, early tomorrow morning, we'll have about twenty-four hours to get to the fourth stone. I've not had a reply from the museum yet about the pictures we've got, matching their stone with ours. We can't take the three stones because they'll be confiscated at the airport—dangerous weapons, or something like that. You know what airport restrictions are like. So, the pictures will have to do. And getting to the fourth stone is an issue, as again, I've had no reply from the curator there yet about us getting to it. Like I said, it's in a glass cabinet. And I've to hold it. But the missing link is with Harry. What does that Irish language translate into, with those missing words about what else we might have to do?'

Again we sat silently. Harry came through the kitchen door.

'Think I've got something.'

'What is it?' I questioned.

'Pretty much the word "held". Doesn't mean a lot yet, but definitely the word "held" is mentioned. Could be you hold something, Laura, probably the stone, in a certain way. We know that already, but it's a start. I'll plough on; let you know.'

He walked out of the kitchen back to the living room as quickly as he'd come in, seeming like a man possessed, I thought.

All three of us stared at each other.

'Held? Held the stone, Jack? In a particular way?' said Laura.

'I reckon that's probably it. Well, we did know that already. That could be all it is? What d' you think, Mum?'

'Well, give it some more time. It seems likely, though I'm sure there's more to it than that. Harry's got the rest of this afternoon before you get your flight tonight. Just wait and see.'

'You're right. Let's just wait and see, shall we, Laura?' I said, looking at her.

'Yes. Time. He needs time to crack this code. Although it seems too simple to only be me just holding the stone.'

So, we sat in the kitchen, waiting until the early evening, when we'd have to make our way to the airport occasionally popping into Harry to see if we could see anything in the copied pages of the book, he couldn't.

17. Off to New York.

For the rest of that sixth day, Harry studied the copies of the book, trying to decipher more words and letters. He'd managed to understand individual letters, he said, including an o, an r, and an m. The problem was that there were gaps in between these letters. It was now guess work as to what it all said.

So, later that evening, it was time to leave for the airport.

'Harry, you're getting weary. You've been at this since late morning, when we got back from the shop. Are you going to be okay taking us to the airport?' I said; we were alone in the living room.

'Absolutely. This is like trying to make words up from missing letters. You know I always liked crossword puzzles.'

'And you need to be fresh to look at crosswords. No matter what, I'll never be able to thank you enough,' I said, out of earshot of Laura, not wanting her to think I was being pessimistic.

'I'll get it, Jack. I will.'

'That I'm confident of. Now, though, we need to get to the airport. Then you can get back and sleep, fresh for another look at the book's pages, see if you can't find out the last piece of the jigsaw for us, okay?'

'Okay.'

Laura came in from the kitchen then. She'd been tidying up with Mum.

'I heard you. Time to go, I think, you two,' she said, yawning as she finished speaking.

'Well, that's a first lately. You feeling tired?' I asked.

'Been feeling strange, Jack. Don't know why. It's like the energy has started being sapped from me since this afternoon. It could be linked to the fact that there's a full moon due, and were getting closer to the seventh day.'

'Maybe. Your energy levels aren't what they've been for the last few days, then?'

'No. You see any reason why in the book at all, Harry? Does it explain anything in there as to why I'm getting weary?'

'Afraid not. Seen nothing like that. Not in the other pages at all, even those I know about. Could be linked to the full moon, though, draining you. You look more pale now, Laura,' he said, glancing up at her from the pages of the Book of Scrolls spread on the table.

She looked into the living room mirror for a few seconds before replying. 'You're right Harry. What d'you think, Jack? More pale?'

'To be honest, yes. Don't like to say it, but yep. I'm really concerned about you now, Laura. Don't want to lose you again.'

I walked over to her at the mirror and held her tightly, not wanting to let her go ever again. We kissed, neither of us caring that Harry was sitting a mere couple of metres from us. We had no time for embarrassment now. As our lips parted, we still held each other, and Harry got up from sitting at the table, and stretched his body, putting his arms up in the air.

'Right. I'm ready. Let's get going,' he said.

'Your flight's just before midnight, Jack, isn't it?' questioned Mum, who'd been in the kitchen, but came into the living room as Laura and I were still standing in front of the mirror.

'Yep,' I replied.

'Seven o'clock now, so you all get yourselves going early right now, just in case there's any traffic problems. I'll have an early night and say goodbye right now. You've got your keys, Harry, just let yourself in when you return.'

Mum hugged Harry after he'd finished stretching to wake himself up after studying the photos for hours; she said to him, 'Drive safely. Don't rush, you've got plenty of time to get to the airport now. It's a good idea to go early, all of you.'

Then she turned to Laura. They looked at each other in silence for a few moments before Mum spoke again.

'Listen. I can feel what you're going through, you know that. I believe it'll all work out. Keep believing yourself, Laura. You must continue to have faith too— although there's not much time, there is time enough.'

They embraced each other then. I could see that they didn't want to let go of each other. It could be the last time they ever saw each other, although I truly hoped it wouldn't be.

'I believe. I really, truly do. Thank you,' Laura said, as they held each other closely, until Mum eased her hold and they both turned towards me.

'Jack. Oh, Jack.' Mum could say nothing else. She started to cry then. I reached out to her and held her tightly in my arms before speaking. 'Mum, it'll work. I've got the faith. From you. And from Harry. I'll never stop believing.' I didn't cry. I knew I had to stay strong right then, for all of our sakes. Our embrace eased.

'Okay, then. Off you go. I love you all. Bags packed and ready to go?' Mum said, in a faltering, stuttering voice full of emotion.

'Yep. All under control, Mum,' replied Harry, in his ever calm voice.

He took the keys to our car from the bureau before going upstairs to the toilet. Mum said goodbye one more time following Harry upstairs to bed. She looked exhausted and was indeed having an early night like she'd said. I went to go and collect our case and bags from the bedroom, as we'd packed all we thought we'd need earlier in the afternoon.

'Good night to you all. Safe journey, you two. Just keep believing. My love is with you, always,' said Mum, as she went into her bedroom, clearly exhausted by her ordeal. I hugged her once more—saying nothing— hoping myself that I would see her again, and soon.

I made my way downstairs with our luggage, waiting for Harry to come back down, checking that we had the print out for the flights and our passports before Laura spoke quietly to me.

'Every day we've had together has been a good day, Jack. Apart from one hour at the train station. I don't know why it's us who this has happened to, but it is. So no regrets. Not now I've got you again. And it'll be for good.'

We kissed then and held each other, and I realised we'd not told Harry or Mum exactly where the museum was before I spoke. 'Never any regrets with you. And hey, they don't know where we're going exactly, do they?' I whispered into her ear as we continued holding each other closely.

'No, they don't.'

'Just in case, we need to let them know, don't we?'

'Yes, you're right, Jack. I feel like I'm losing some of my efficient self since yesterday. Sorry,' she said loosening her grip around my body.

'Don't be daft. I think it's got something to do with the full moon,' I said, knowing that she needed some reassurance right now.

Nodding at her, I decided to go into the kitchen to get some paper to write a note for Mum and Harry.

Dear Mum and Harry,

We both want to say that no words can thank you both enough for what you've done. In case anything does go wrong, here's the address of the museum in New York. You know the place from the details Laura found on the internet, and the fourth stone is there. Think you know this already anyway, Harry.

But, if anything happens, you'll need to know where to come to get us. I hope, we hope, and don't think that's going to be the case. Neither of us do.

However, in case an explanation is needed—especially about Laura—then this is where we're going:

The Metropolitan Museum
On Museum Mile
Manhattans Upper East Side
Next to Central Park

1000 Fifth Avenue
New York
If this works out, then we'll be in touch, but we won't know when, knowing we've got to be somewhere else in the world.

You have my number Harry. Call any time, I'll know it's you. We shall always be grateful for this chance. We love you.

Jack and Laura. XX

Coming back into the living room from the kitchen where I'd written the note, I gave it to Laura to read. She read it in silence, and nodded to me afterwards, tears welling up in her eyes. I took it from her and put it in the bureau for safe keeping, inside an envelope with their names on it, intending to tell Harry about it when we got to the airport.

Just as I closed the bureau, Harry came downstairs and we waited in the living room.

'I said goodbye to Mum, she's fallen asleep already.' Harry said.

'Good. Maybe she'll get back to her usual self once the ageing has finished and she's got used to her changed body,' I replied.

Harry, in the meantime, picked up the old spyglass on the table to have another look at the pages of the book before we departed for the airport, and said, 'Let's just wait and see, Jack. Let's just wait and see.'

Laura and I stood either side of him as he studied the pages once again, all of us silent for a minute or so. *Maybe we could help?* I thought.

'Would it be useful if either of us had another look?' I said.

'Well, the only person who understands the Gaelic language here, other than myself, is Mum, actually. But you know some words and phrases Jack, don't you?'

'Yep, got a vague memory of reading the Irish language when I was a boy.'

'By all means, have a look, both of you. Tell you what, let's take the pages with us in the car. I'm driving so you two have a look on the way to the airport, as time's flying by. Oops! No pun intended there!'

We all smiled before Laura spoke. 'C'mon then, let's get into the car. We'll have a look on the way.'

I put the pages into the folder I'd taken from the shop, and grabbed the spyglass as we all left the cottage quietly, for the journey to the airport.

So that we could look at the pages, we both sat in the back seat of our car, as Harry drove.

There were four pages, in different sizes; they were the ones we'd copied in the shop. They had words that I knew, vaguely recognisable as an ancient Irish language, but I didn't fully understand them. I knew odd words and letters from Mum telling us as kids, and us hearing them. But seeing them, I had no idea what they meant as I looked closely. The problem was that—as Harry had said—the page was damaged with some of the letters being unreadable. I knew he was right when he said it'd be guess work as I looked at the pages through the spyglass, hoping that an old memory would be jogged in me.

'Hey, you've got this one word already, haven't you? The one that translates to "held",' I said. 'I can't see in the other letters after that, any that look the same as the word "held" in the translation. So, by process of elimination, none of those other letters and words that are legible look like those letters that make up the word "held".'

'And what are you getting at, Jack?' said Harry, as he drove along the motorway.

'Well, that tells me—don't know about you—that the other letters that are readable, have got to be something, other than h, e, l, or d, maybe?'

'Of course. I can maybe count those four letters out of it. Although they could be some of the letters that are unreadable. But that's good, Jack. It's a help. I'll keep looking at it when I get back. Thanks.'

It was something that could be nothing, I thought to myself. But it might help. Laura looked at me and smiled. It was that smile that I knew was only for me. She was looking tired herself, as we snuggled up closer to each other in the car, still looking at the pages for any more clues.

The remainder of the journey was fine, though we'd found no other clues as to what the missing words could or couldn't be in the copies of the pages of The Book of Scrolls.

We were early when Harry dropped us off. When we got out of the car, he said, 'Don't forget. Leave your mobile phone on. I'll call or text you with anything. Any little thing. I'll keep working on it until tomorrow night.'

'Thanks. You're the best brother any man could ever have, Harry. Hope I see you again.'

'You will, Jack.'

Embracing once more, I hugged him as tightly as I could until Laura got out of the car and approached us. When I let go of Harry for the last time, walking to the back of the car to get our bags out, I tried my hardest to stay in control of my emotions, but it was difficult knowing I may not ever see him again and, more importantly, nor might Laura. I breathed deeply as I took the bags from the boot of the car, stifling tears, trying to stay strong.

Laura said, with tears in her eyes once again, and a croaky voice. 'Thanks for everything, Harry. We know this'd never have happened if not for you. And I agree with, Jack. If I had a brother, I'd want him to be like you. Oh, and we've agreed that, whatever happens, our car is yours now.'

'Thanks, Laura,' he replied. They hugged while I stood with the bags in my hands. It felt good that they got on so well. They'd got to know each other when we were younger, of course.

'Off you go, go on. Before I get a parking ticket! For my new car!' Harry said, smiling, as Laura walked towards me. I could see tears on his cheeks as he spoke those words with an emotional, croaky voice.

'Oh, and we've left a letter for you and Mum in the cottage,' I shouted over the din and hubbub. 'Just in case, I've written the name and address of the museum for you. Left it in the bureau with yours and Mum's names on an envelope. Thanks Harry, for everything.'

Walking towards us both again, hugging us as one, he whispered to us both, 'Make it work, make it work. I don't want to lose you guys, never ever.' I could hear his voice trembling as he said these words. We all knew now how important this really was.

He kissed us both on our cheeks, smiled, and turned away, getting back into the car. He drove off, sticking his hand out of the window to wave goodbye. We both looked at each other and smiled. No need for any words. We walked into the airport, looking for the check-in. Finally, we found it, wandering around the giant concourse of the airport, and booked in. We knew that we had a few hours to kill waiting for take-off. So we strolled around the shops for a while, grabbing a sandwich and drink after we'd gone through security, waiting to be called for our flight.

Later, as we boarded the plane for take-off, I checked my phone for any message from Harry, as I'd done several times already. One missed call and one message! What with all of the noise at the airport, I'd not heard it. I showed it to Laura after reading it, before I had to turn it to silent.

Tried calling you. Got back and Mum was in bed. Cottage been burgled! She doesn't know. Nothing seems missing, but NO letter in bureau for us, with papers all over the place. Sorry to say only one person it's likely to be. Not sure what he's planning on doing. If I get any info, I'll call or text a.s.a.p.

BE CAREFUL.

Harry. Xx

Neither of us said anything after she read the message. We'd have to wait until we landed in New York now, to try and contact Harry.

18. Harry's warning.

The flight went smoothly. Eventually, we both fell asleep, cat napping throughout. Exhaustion hadn't set in, but we knew it was taking its toll on us both. When we started to make our approach for landing, Laura, still half asleep, said, 'What'll we do about the message when we get there?'

'I hope your dad's not going to try and follow us. The message said the cottage had been broken into. Why would anyone want to do that? I know Mum's got things in the parlour, but it's not common knowledge, plus everything's insured. Nothing's missing, he said. Apart from the letter and papers all over the place from the bureau. Obviously only one person, I'm sad to say.'

'When you came back from the shop, you said Dad was angry with you and Harry. What if he'd shut the shop and followed you? Broken in after we'd left, before Harry got back? Dad would've waited for your mother to be out of sight. He'd never hurt her.'

'Sounds possible. But he's no chance of getting to us here. I wouldn't have thought there were any flights with available seating to get him here in time.'

'Thing is Jack, that may not bother him. He's blamed you throughout. If he thinks I'll never come back, all he'll want to do is get you. He won't care about the consequences. He must be obsessed.'

'Well, let's not think about it until we've landed. When we're there, I'll get hold of Harry, find out exactly what he knows about this. By then, he may have checked the shop to see if your dad closed it or not, and he might—more importantly—have got a bit further with the book translation.'

The sign went on to fasten seat belts for landing then. So, with the noise droning in our ears, we sat quietly until we landed. Safely.

When we were on the ground and got off the plane, we got directions from airport staff for the car hire place. I called Harry. It took five attempts to get through to him. But eventually, he answered the phone.

'Harry, that you?'

It was a bad line. Not surprising, I thought, as I was calling all the way from America. I checked my watch. It said eight o'clock, but that couldn't be right, it was dark here now, I thought to myself.

'It's me, Jack. You landed. Both okay?'

'Yep, we're here. What's gone on at the cottage? Your message said a break-in and a letter missing.'

'That's right. No letter from you. You'll have to let me know which museum the stone is at.'

'The Metropolitan Museum, Manhattan.'

'Right. Okay. I'll make a note of it. Now listen, Jack, you've not got a lot of time, so I'll make this quick.'

'Go ahead, we're listening.'

'When I got back from the airport, the front door was locked as normal. I can only presume whoever it was— and I think we know who—had a key. Maybe a spare from Laura, possibly? I don't know.' He paused.

'Carry on, Harry,' I said.

'Well, I went into the cottage, and I saw papers in the living room all over the floor. The bureau was open, with odd letters and forms all over the place. I checked on Mum, and she was sound asleep still. Thank God Mum's okay. Fortunately we took the photos of the book with us in the car. So I've still got them to study, now I'm back.'

'Yep, that's really good Mum's fine. Okay. Now, you found no letter that I'd left? The one I'd addressed to you and Mum together? I put it in a white envelope, thanking you both for everything and leaving the address of the museum. I left it in the bureau, where I told you, when you dropped us off at the airport.'

'No letter, Jack. Not addressed to me and Mum.'

'Shit!' I shouted down the phone, and Laura stared at me open-mouthed, having heard all of the conversation.

There was silence on the line for a few moments whilst I was thinking about what to say. It was a crackly reception, but we could hear and understand each other.

'Right, no police, Harry. We can't have them involved. And the front door's not been broken. He must've had a spare key. I remember leaving one at his house for Laura years ago, before we moved into the flat.' Laura nodded at me when I said this to Harry.

'Wasn't planning on contacting them, anyway.'

'Good. Can you see if he's at his house? Or if he's at the shop? Don't s'pose you'd been to check after you'd got back and found the cottage in a mess, whether he'd closed the shop or not?'

'Already ahead of you. After I'd got to the cottage, I tried calling you, but you didn't answer.'

'Yep, sorry, missed the call at the airport with all the racket and noise. But I saw your text just as we were boarding the plane.'

'Well, what I did once I'd got back from the airport and found the cottage in a mess, was to go straight round to Dempsey's house. There was no sign of him, so I went round the back to look, as well. And his car wasn't there either.'

'What about the shop, Harry? What time did you get there?'

'Not sure, but it was close to midnight here. It was closed, obviously, at that time of night.'

'Yep, understandable.'

'But when I got there, a notice was on the door, saying it was closed for three days due to stock taking.'

'What! We've never done that.'

'Didn't think so, Jack.'

'Oh my God! He's not going to try and follow us, surely?' shouted Laura.

Harry could hear that easily on the phone as well, before he spoke again.

'Don't know. But you two had better be careful from here on in. Listen, you know after we saw him in the morning at the shop, he had a lot of rage and anger inside him. Could be he shut the shop then, before we'd left, and was watching us. He knew you'd be going today. Time's running out y'know.'

'Yep, we know it. Must be about eight o'clock in the morning there Harry, isn't it? That's what my watch says. Well, we've found where the hire car company is, and we're off to find the museum. Mind you, it's not open until the morning, isn't that right, Laura?'

She leant towards the phone to speak to Harry while I held it still. 'That's right, Harry, opens at ten o'clock in the morning until five thirty in the evening, so we've got all day to get to the stone.'

'Good. Well, I'd better let you go. And that's the right time here, Jack. But be careful. Take care. And remember you're on New York time now. Check what time it is there. I think it's about five or six hours behind us in the UK. So maybe that'll help you.'

'Will do, Harry. You take care. Let me know if you find out anything about the words in the book.'

'OK. Bye for now. Love to you both. We'll talk again before tonight.'

'Thanks, Harry. Bye.'

The phone line went dead. I looked at Laura.

'Did you know that, Laura, about the time? I didn't even think of that.'

'Neither did I. Didn't think about that, it never crossed my mind. Sorry.'

'We're both sorry, I never thought about it at all. Don't know why. But at least it gives us a few more hours to get to the museum. Only problem is, if your dad does try to get here to stop us, it gives him more time as well.'

'I know that now. C'mon, let's get to the hire car place and get moving. The internet stated they've got a map, and it's only about an hour or so to drive from here.'

You want some food first, or shall we just go?' I asked.

'Could do with a bite to eat. Let's get out of this airport first and get on the road to the museum in Manhattan; we'll find a place nearby. This is s'posed to be a twenty-four hour town, so should be no problem finding a place to eat, have a coffee maybe.'

'Good. Let's go.'

We were still in the JFK airport area. There were signs for the subway, air trains and a taxi rank. Having been pointed in the direction of these signs by airport staff, I asked a security guard if we were in the right area to collect our hire car. We were. It was just around the next building.

Once we'd sorted out the relevant paperwork, we got the keys to the car, with instructions inside it regarding the remote control key fob, as well as a pamphlet regarding care when driving on the New York highways.

So, we got in the car, and found signs on the pamphlet to Central Park. That was the first place we'd need to recognise, knowing that it'd give us a bearing to find Museum Mile. Obviously, not having driven in America before, I knew they drove on the other side of the road. So I'd have to keep my wits about me.

'Hey, we didn't check the time, Jack. Did you hear it on the plane announcement when we landed?'

'No, I didn't. You're right. Put the radio on, let's see if they give a time, or if it's got a clock on the dashboard somewhere.'

We both checked the dashboard before we drove away from the airport. I checked the controls before driving off, wanting to try and familiarise myself with the car. There was a clock, and then when Laura tuned in the car radio, a voice came on saying almost the exact same time as the clock in the car. It was 3.22 a.m. It was no surprise we were both tired. My watch said eight thirty in the morning, so New York time was behind, like Harry had said.

'C'mon, set your watch, Jack, I've changed mine now. We need to know the correct time.'

'Done,' I replied, adjusting the time on my watch.

The engine I'd already started, so we made our way out of the airport parking area, heading up the boulevard, where we saw a sign for Central Park. I'd never seen so many signs, nor lanes on a motorway—or a highway, as they call them here in America. But I knew that's where we needed to go. Road signs were in green, and this first one we saw said forty kilometres. That'd take just an hour or so if we kept to the speed limit, no problem.

'Not too far to drive, baby. If we see a café on the way, we'll pull over for some food. You got any US Dollars, Jack?'

'Er, no.'

'Lucky I've got some, then, isn't it,' she said, turning to smile at me.

'Hmm. On the ball, aren't you?'

'I do try. Your mother got them for me yesterday.'

We both smiled. I could see her out of the corner of my eye and as I drove down the highway, I said, 'Now, eyes peeled for a café; got to be an all-night one open along here soon.'

Sure enough, after taking almost half an hour getting out of the airport—and taking a couple of wrong turns as it was so busy—we were on the highway, and Laura spotted a big café in the distance.

'Up there Jack, take your time and pull over. We can get something to eat. I'm really hungry, even after the meal on the flight. How about you?'

'Yep, starving actually.'

So, I turned off the highway, pulled up, and parked. We were outside a café with an enormous red fluorescent light advertising the name *Big Momma's*. Although we'd had food on the plane, we'd only eaten some toast earlier in the day at Mum's cottage, and a sandwich. Neither of us ate all of our meals on board the flight, as we didn't fancy it at the time. So, with Laura looking pale and her make-up looking like it was wearing off as we sat in the car, I said, 'You don't look so pale now, but I think a top-up of your make-up is in order as well as food, don't you?'

'Think you're right there,' she said, looking in her sun visor mirror.

'Right. C'mon, let's get into the café, I'll ask for the toilet or restroom, and then you can pop in to put some face paint on. Keep that tan topped up!'

'Will do, Doctor Stanton!'

We laughed a tired laugh as we both got out of the car and walked into the café. It was empty, other than two chaps sitting on stools, drinking coffee at the long bar in what looked like blue uniforms. I saw NYPD on their epaulettes. Had to be police, I thought to myself.

'What d'you fancy to eat? Anything? What about a cooked breakfast, seeing as its gone way past four in the morning here now?' I said, opening the door to the café for her.

'Sounds good. I'm starving. That'll do, with coffee. Here, I've got one hundred dollars, that'll be plenty to get the food, and more petrol, and entry to the museum.'

'Good. Efficiency returned, huh?'

'Getting there, Jack. Getting there, again.'

'I'll go and order.'

We kissed and then she walked off to the toilet. I went to the counter, and ordered the food and coffee, waiting for her to return. I knew she'd be a while, especially having to put that make-up on, so I went and sat down at a table that looked towards the restroom, waiting for Laura to come out.

As I waited, a waitress came over with a pot of coffee. I said to her, 'Thank you.'

'Is that an English accent, sir?' she said, in her own soft American accent.

'Yes, it is.'

'Well, you all have a nice stay here in America. I see your young lady's popped to the restroom. She's been a while. You want me to check on her?'

'That's very nice of you. I'm sure she's fine, though we've had a long journey.'

'It's no trouble, sir,' she said again, in her soft accent.

'That's kind of you. Thanks.'

She left the pot of coffee on the table and went into the ladies toilets. Moments later, she rushed out.

'Sir! Sir! Your wife, she's collapsed in the restroom!'

I was out of the seat like a shot, the waitress' shouting having woken me up, as I had started to doze off with tiredness.

No! Laura, collapsed!

I rushed into the restroom to see her on the floor. I was instantly horrified. But, I thought quickly.

'Can you get me a glass of water please, waitress?' I shouted.

'Straight away,' she replied, dashing out of the room, quick as a flash.

I dropped to the floor, putting my hand gently behind Laura's head, and by the time I'd done this, the waitress had returned with a jug of water and a glass. I had the feeling of being here before, holding Laura in my arms. I knew exactly what that feeling was. I didn't like it. It did not feel good.

'Here you are, sir.'

I put my hand into the jug, and literally threw a handful of water onto Laura's face. I wasn't sure what to do. But it worked. Within a few seconds, she opened her eyes, staring up at me.

'Laura? You okay, baby?'

'Er, Jack? What's going on? I walked into the toilet and now you're here. Did I faint?'

'Yes you did. Luckily, the waitress came in to check on you.'

'I'm Connie. Thought you'd been in the restroom for a while, so I said I'd come and check you were okay.

Thank goodness I did, I found you on the floor. You were out for the count.'

Laura stared at me, then the waitress we knew now as Connie.

'Here, have a drink of water,' I said, as Connie passed a glass to me. 'You're probably dehydrated. And we both need to eat. Sorry I splashed water over you.'

She smiled, then sipped some water before I continued.

'Seems like you fainted. I'm on the ground with you, like a couple of weeks ago. For a split second I thought I'd lost you again.'

All of a sudden, Laura looked me straight in the eyes. The bleary dazed look she had vanished in an instant. 'No chance, Jack Stanton. I'm going to be Mrs Stanton, you try and stop me. Or Mrs something else, who knows what?'

The waitress stared at us. 'You folks all right? You want the emergency services?'

'No, we'll be fine. Just need some food. We've had a long journey today,' said Laura.

'Funny, that's what your husband said earlier. You people read each other's minds, or something?'

'Not exactly. But we could use your help, Connie. D'you mind if we call you Connie?'

'Oh? No, please do. It's my name after all,' she said, pointing to the badge on her uniform. 'Now, come on, let's get you off the floor, seated down, and get some food inside you. Both of you. Are you hurt at all, Laura?'

'No, I'm okay, Connie, I'm not in any pain. I remember feeling faint and falling onto my knees, before passing out. But I'm okay, thank you.'

'Yes, once we've eaten—and we both need a meal right now—could you point us in the direction of a particular New York museum?' I asked.

'Sure. No problem, sir. Let's get you off the floor, young lady.'

'Please, call me Jack. You know this is Laura,' I said as Connie helped me to get Laura to her feet, sitting her on a stool. 'You feeling any better now?' I questioned her, as we helped her to sit down.

'Yes. Really, I am. Just a bit de-hydrated and I need a meal. Think I could have some more of that water please, not in my face, but to drink. Then I'll get myself sorted out.' She smiled again, as she began to dab her face with a tissue.

'Yep, sorry,' I replied, filling a glass for her.

'I'll stay with you and make sure you don't faint again. Want to make sure you're safe in our café,' said Connie.

'No, that's fine, I'll be okay now.' Then she gulped that full glass of water I'd poured for her, in one go.

'Can't do that, I'm afraid,' said Connie. 'Orders of the café. I'm staying, no arguments.'

'Thank you. That's really kind of you. Jack, get back to our seats and have a coffee. I'll be fine. Really.'

'You sure?'

'Yes. Go on. I'll be five minutes. Don't worry.'

'All right, as long as you're sure. I don't want to leave you alone like this.'

'I'll be fine. Connie's going to help, aren't you? And I've got to put my make-up on, seeing as I've had water thrown all over my face, by you!'

We all laughed, me with embarrassment. It'd been some time since I'd felt the heat rise in my face. But I didn't care, as long as she was okay right now.

'Now, you're Laura and you're Jack. Is that right?' Connie replied, questioningly.

'Yes, Connie. He's Jack. We're going to get married soon.'

'That's nice. Now listen, Jack. I'll make sure Laura's fine and dandy. You go and take a seat. I promise I'll get her refreshed and back to you in a few minutes. Women's stuff, you know?'

'Thank you, Connie. That's very kind.'

I smiled at them both. Laura gave me one of those big smiles back. Then I turned and walked out of the ladies restroom as she poured herself another glass of water. Luckily it was the early hours of the morning, and nobody else went in to use it.

Making my way back to our seats, I felt relief. One of the guys at the counter asked if everything was okay in the restroom, as did the chap making our breakfasts. I thanked them and told them she was okay, but tired from a long journey. Fortunately, they seemed to accept my explanation of the situation. The guys at the counter were indeed NYPD officers, which I noticed now more distinctly as I sat down, seeing their blue and white police car outside. I didn't want to attract any more attention to us than we'd had already, so I sat quietly, pouring myself a coffee before Laura returned.

A few minutes later, she walked out of the restroom with the waitress behind her, sitting down, and having a coffee straight away, and then another glass of water. And after a few minutes, she had another coffee. I watched her, realising that she had been badly dehydrated.

Shortly after seeing her gulp down her coffee, our food arrived, courtesy of Connie. It was the biggest plate of all day or night breakfast I'd ever seen. Absolutely enormous! I'd heard stories of big meals in America but, never having been there before, couldn't believe how much food was served up on our plates!

'Thank you, Connie.'

'It's a pleasure, sir. I mean, Jack. Now, you both eat up, looks like you both need a hearty meal. Enjoy. You feeling better now, Laura?'

'Yes, thanks for your help in the toilets, er, I mean, restroom. When we've finished eating, we'll come and have a chat with you, if that's okay.'

'Sure thing, honey. I'll pop over to you.'

She turned and walked away, and Laura said to me, 'She's been so nice. And really helpful. Plus, she can help us find the museum with any luck. I asked her if she'd heard of it when she waited for me in the toilet. But I only put a little make-up on. Felt my colour coming back to me.'

'Well, that's good she might be able to help. And don't worry about the make-up, you don't actually look as pale now. Might be to do with being nearer the fourth stone? Now, c'mon, eat. We both need a meal.'

'Will do.'

And she did look better, I thought to myself. It could be that, now we were here and getting closer to the fourth stone, it was helping Laura.

We sat and ate our meal quietly, neither of us speaking for the next fifteen minutes or so. Connie the waitress left us alone until we'd finished our meal. She must've sensed we were enjoying it.

Then she came over, didn't say a word, smiled and got us another pot of coffee whilst we were still eating. I'd never experienced service like this anywhere. I hoped everything was going to work out for us.

When we'd finally finished, Connie came over again. Behind her were the two police officers, who'd been at the counter drinking coffee.

One of them said, 'You folks okay now? You feeling better now, miss? Need any help with where you're going? We can help, if you need it,' he said, looking at Laura before pointing to his badge.

'That's very kind of you, officer. Thank you, but we'll be fine now, thank you again.'

'Okay ma'am. And you, sir. Enjoy your stay in New York. Have a nice day when daylight creeps upon us. Take care,' he said, smiling, and he and the other officer nodded at us, as they stood at our table.

'Thanks again. Much appreciated,' I replied, and as they made their way out of Big Momma's café doors, Connie began to speak to us.

'Looks like you both enjoyed that meal. More coffee, Laura?'

'No thanks, Connie. I'm contented now, thank you.'

'And you, Jack? More coffee?' Connie said, smiling at me.

'Not for me, Connie. Could we have the bill please? And thanks again for all of your help earlier.'

'Nice people like you folks from England need a good first impression of us New Yorkers. Is it your first time here, both of you?'

'Yes, it is,' I replied.

'Well, I'll clear your table, then pop back with your bill. And you wanted directions to a museum, I recall?' she said, looking at Laura.

'Please, if it's not too much trouble,' Laura replied.

'No trouble at all. Give me a few minutes, my shift finishes soon, so I'll come and sit with you and give you directions to the museum. It's quietened down in here tonight, so I should be able to clock off work early.'

'Connie. How can we thank you? You've been so nice to us.'

'Well Laura, as we say here in the US of A, "Have a nice day". But you two just have a good time while you're here. And you never know, you might like it so much you might come back.'

'Thanks again, Connie,' Laura replied, smiling up at her.

She walked away with the dishes, leaving us alone for a few minutes before she returned.

When she did, she'd got another pot of coffee, three cups, and our bill, which I read and paid with some of the money Laura had given me earlier.

'Thank you,' said Connie. 'I'll sort out the bill while you pour the coffee for all three of us. My shift's over now, almost, so I'll be back in a few minutes to help you folks out.'

'Thanks, Connie,' we both replied simultaneously, smiling at each other as we did.

As I poured the coffee into three cups, Laura looked at me before speaking.

'More coffee? Well, we'll have to drink it,' she said, smiling, before continuing. 'Like it here, don't you, Jack?'

'Actually, I do. I'm feeling relaxed, even though we've not reached the end yet, as there's more to do.'

'Strange how she thought we'd maybe read each other's minds earlier, when we'd both said separately about our journey.'

'Hmm. Wonder where she lives, if it's anywhere near the museum?'

'D' you think we're giving out too much information? Should we keep ourselves to ourselves a bit more?' questioned Laura.

'Well, if we do that, it'd make us look suspicious. Let's just go with the flow here, she seems nice and genuine.'

'Yep, I think you're right. Nice lady. But don't tell her what we're planning to do, will you?'

'Don't be daft. Not telling anybody about that, other than the museum curator, or whatever they're called here, when we get there later today.'

'Here she comes,' whispered Laura.

Connie sat down with us at the table. She looked in her mid-forties, with dark skin and blond hair tied up in a bun, not as tall as Laura, and not as slim either. She'd changed her red work jacket to a casual blue cardigan, I noticed, as she sat next to Laura on the bench seat.

'Okay you two. Where d'you want to get to? I'm a native here in New York, live on the upper east side of Manhattan. Bit of a trek from here y'know. Got to get back for my two kids by seven o'clock this morning, got a babysitter there now. So, time to spare, as it's about a forty minute or so drive from here.'

I thought to myself, as I glanced at Laura, that she had to be for real, being so open about everything. My instincts I hoped, would be right.

'Well, Connie, Jack and I need to get to a museum in New York, it's called the Metropolitan Museum, in Fifth Avenue. Any idea which route to take, which'll get us there for opening time today?'

'Oh sure. That's a piece of cake! No problem to find. The Met's what you need. Beautiful building. My kids have been there on school trips, we live about twenty minutes away ourselves.'

'Sounds promising, Connie.'

'Sure, I know exactly where it is. Now, I don't know what you do, but I'd guess that arriving this time of the morning you might not just be sightseers. But that's not my business. You both seem like real nice people. Luckily, I'm driving that way shortly, but I turn off, like I said, twenty minutes or so before arriving there. I'll tell you where to go. No, tell you what, I'll draw it on this napkin here. That'll be easier for you.'

She took a napkin, having a pen in her pocket. Then she proceeded to draw a map of where we were and how to get to the Metropolitan Museum. I knew it was probably right, as she'd written down that we needed to drive down Museum Mile, which was next to Central Park. I remembered that from writing the letter to Mum and Harry, as I had the exact address written in my diary and phone, too. When she finished drawing her map, she pushed it towards us. I leant forward to have a look. It didn't look too complicated.

'Thanks, Connie. That's great.' Said Laura.

'No problem, honey. You and your man could be archaeologists, scientists, or graduates for all I know. But I know people. And you are both good people. That's all I need to know right now. Have a look at my map. Any questions, fire away.'

We all sat silently after she said this, as we studied her makeshift map. Connie nodded at me before speaking. Then she put her arm around Laura, still sitting next to her.

'Whatever it is, you'll work it out. Have faith. It'll work.'

She didn't know how close I was to spilling the beans then. I wanted to tell her why we were going there. But I put my hand to my mouth, gently scratching my chin to cover up my sigh as I coughed and breathed heavily, before she continued.

'Right then. Now, finish your coffee, jump in your car in a few minutes, and follow me to where I've shown you on my fabulous map! Then, when we get to my turning at the upper-eastside, you can carry on following my directions; are you okay with that?'

'Will do, Connie. Can we thank you, in any way?' I questioned.

She held her hand up in front of both of us. 'Hey, you kids just do what you've to do. Like I say, I don't need to know. Just glad to help a couple of souls, lost, on their way. Now come on, let's get going.'

She stood up, finishing her coffee as we both just sipped some of ours. Then we left the café. Her car was parked a few spaces away from ours, and we walked to hers first.

Laura reached out and hugged Connie. We'd never met her before, but who knew whether we'd meet her again. When Laura let her go, Connie approached me too and whispered into my ear as she hugged me.

'Jack, my man. She's sweet. You take care of this one, and yourself.'

'I know, Connie. Thanks again. I'll take good care of her.'

She let go of me then. Laura couldn't hear what we'd both whispered to each other. I'd tell her on the way, I thought.

As she got into her car, Connie called over to us both as we were getting into ours, to follow her. 'Maybe I'll convert to checking a museum out, like you two! You come all this way, there's got to be something good there!'

'Maybe, Connie. Maybe. Lead the way for us, please!' said Laura, smiling, turning back to reply to her as we were getting in the car.

'Sure thing, honey. Follow me to the turn off on your map. And good luck to the pair of you.'

Driving out of the parking lot, I told Laura what Connie had whispered to me.

'Really nice woman. Seems like she's had things tough. Be nice to help her in some way, if we ever could, Jack, don't you think?'

'Yep. Put that one in the memory bank. Right now, let's follow her. We've got to be somewhere, and now time's important. We need to get there first, to form a plan. And let's hope there's no outside interference, if you know what I mean?'

'I do. And I hope I get to say those two words, for real, soon, Jack.'

'You will. I hope so too. Don't know where, but, we'll make it happen.'

Then, as we drove down the massive highway of lanes towards the museum, I glanced at Laura. Her colour was definitely not anywhere near as pale as yesterday. The meal might've helped, but it could've been getting nearer to the fourth stone, like I'd thought earlier.

'How're you feeling now?' I asked her.

'Better. Mightn't have been the healthiest meal, but I needed that. Sorry about fainting. I just needed fluid and food. Hadn't drunk much yesterday when looking at those photos with Harry, nor at the airport either. I'd not noticed with one thing and another. Sorry, baby. I'm good now. Feeling much better. Now, follow that car!'

We both laughed. We were in America. New York.

'That's what they say in the movies!' I said, laughing.

'Just couldn't resist that,' she said, laughing.

Laura looked better than she had a couple of hours ago. Her colour was getting almost back to normal quickly, with very little make-up assistance. I wondered how Mum was doing now, as I drove, not speaking for a few minutes.

'Don't worry about your mother, Jack. I'm sure she's going to be fine. Harry's with her. They'll be alright. Got to concentrate on us now.'

She was right, and so perceptive of my thoughts. There was another silence in the car for a few minutes, neither of us speaking as I followed Connie in her car, wondering if Laura had read my thoughts about Mum.

'You really do know me, so well. I think we'll like it here in New York. What d'you think?' I said, breaking our comfortable silence.

'Well, despite Harry's warning about Dad, there's nothing he can do. Surely he can't get here in time to try anything stupid? We just need to know what that page says other than the word "held". He'll come up trumps. He's got to. I want to spend the rest of my life with you Jack, anywhere. But, this'll be a good start. A very good, new start for us.'

She put the radio on in the car then. It was a country and western station, mellow, sedate music for this early hour of the morning. We sat quietly, driving along slowly for the next ten or fifteen minutes or so. It wouldn't be daylight for another couple of hours, so we'd time on our hands to formulate our plan. Laura fell asleep in the car before I saw Connie turn off. I flashed my headlights at her car to say thank you as she turned off the main highway.

Now it was almost five thirty in the morning, and we were driving on Fifth Avenue. In the distance I could see a sign saying Museum Mile. Almost there. Then, as I drove along, I saw it. The Metropolitan Museum. It was an enormous building. We'd arrived.

We were now on our own. I thought about Dempsey breaking in to the cottage, and Harry's warning on the phone earlier, as Laura dozed next to me in the passenger seat...

19. The museum, waiting.

As I approached The Metropolitan Museum I could see yellow taxi cabs parked outside. There were no parking spaces, so I nudged Laura gently to wake her.

'Hey you. We're here. It's the Met. Look. It's massive.'

Daylight was beginning to form as we drove past slowly. We saw an enormous set of steps leading to a lovely old building with giant pillars. It looked like an English stately home.

'Wow, it's beautiful. Can't we stop?'

'Nowhere to park. See all those taxi cabs there? No parking for us. I'll have to drive around and find a parking place around here. Bound to be loads. Anyway, it's not open yet. When it does, we'll get a leaflet to find out exactly where we've got to go. D'you mind if I have a nap, I'm getting tired myself?'

'Jack, course you can. Get a parking place and I'll sort out a ticket. I'll go and have a wander. It'll be daylight soon. You have a sleep, baby,' she said, gently stroking my face as I drove.

'Thanks,' I said.

'Oh, you've got the money. Give me some, and I'll get a ticket to park for the day. We'll need to be here all day and maybe the night.'

'Then, with luck, for the rest of our lives?'

'Absolutely. One long day to go. I'm feeling better now. You sleep and I'll get a ticket when we stop.'

'No, I'll come with you instead of having a nap, get a ticket first after we've found a parking place. The fresh air should wake me up a bit,' I said, changing my mind knowing we'd not much time left.

'Okay,' she replied.

We found a big multi-storey area, which was about a mile away from our destination, the museum. We walked together in the chilly morning air after we'd parked, finding the machine. It took cash, so we got a ticket for forty-eight hours to cover any eventuality. Going back to the car, I was woken up by the fresh, cold, morning air.

'Not sleepy now, with this cold bracing air,' I said.

'C'mon then, let's have a wander around this Fifth Avenue. Got to be some cafés and bars around here. Need to get some water, Jack. We'll have a look around the museum area, then go in later when it's open. Are you okay with that?'

'Yep, sounds good.'

We left the car and started to walk around the shops and buildings, which were enormous. I'd seen nothing like it. Everything was so big and tall, compared to back home. When we arrived at the museum and walked up the steps to it, security men were guarding the entrance, four of them. We were reading a sign outside showing the opening times, with details about different exhibitions being held inside, when one of the guards came up to speak to us.

'Hi there, can I help you?' he questioned in a strong, deep American accent.

'Yes, we just wanted to check the opening times today. Says it opens at ten a.m. until five-thirty this evening, is that right?' I questioned.

'You guys British?'

'Yes sir, we are,' said Laura.

'Well ma'am, it sure is. Open today, but longer than usual. And it'll be a real busy day.'

'What's going on today then, officer?' questioned Laura.

'Well ma'am, sir. It's the third Monday in January tomorrow and that means it's Martin Luther King Day. There'll be parades and all sorts of processions going on tomorrow. But, it being a Sunday today and all, we'll be real busy here. Always happens. That's why we've got added security working today and tomorrow, just to keep the peace. Going to be a busy couple of days. You folks picked a good time to be here, to celebrate the great man's life. You have days in Britain called Bank Holidays, don't you? It'll be like those.'

'Yes, we do. Thanks for the advice. Much appreciated. Does the museum itself stay open much longer than normal just for today?' Laura enquired.

'Ma'am, tonight it stays open until ten o'clock, but it's not open tomorrow. Closed for the celebration and festivities for the great man. Doesn't say it on the signs, never been a need to do that.'

'Thank you. We'll be back later. Looks like a lovely building,' said Laura.

'It sure is. You all have a good day now, enjoy yourselves.'

'Will do. Hope you don't have to work too hard,' she said.

'We do what we have to, ma'am.'

Turning to walk back down the stairs of the museum, Laura grabbed my hand after doing all the talking with the guard. She pulled at my hand and arm, like she used to do when we were kids. I stared at her.

When we reached the bottom of the steps some distance away she spoke again.

'Right, now we've got more time than we thought. That's good for us. Only trouble is, now that guard guy's seen us, he may take an interest in us.'

'No, he'll see tons of people all day like us.'

'Yes I know. But not British, Jack.'

'Oh. Didn't think about that. Probably not as many of us here as them today. Didn't know anything about it being Martin Luther King Day, did you?'

'No idea whatsoever. Obviously know about him, but not the day when his life was celebrated. Just hope if it's really busy as soon as it opens up, we can get to the fourth stone.'

'Hope so. Let's get away from here, I can see the guard looking our way, there's not many people about yet, and it's not opening time for another few hours,' she said, looking at her watch.

'Walk away. C'mon, let's find a café and have a coffee. I'm not hungry yet after that meal. Let's get some water, like you said earlier. Then I'll need a rest. Probably sit in the car and nod off. We can get back here for mid-day. That gives us plenty of time,' I said.

'Okay. Let's go.'

We walked off up Fifth Avenue, wandering around, finding our bearings. A lot of shops and bars were closed, it being just before six o'clock in the morning. I knew but said nothing, knowing we only had—maybe—just hours left together. Eventually, we found a bar down a side street after walking for about half an hour or so, looking at the incredible size of the buildings. We stopped and had a coffee, bought some water. Half an hour later, we left. I needed to sleep. I think Laura did too.

It was daylight, when Laura made her suggestion.

'Hey, I know we're both tired, but—just in case—can we have a walk around this Central Park?'

'Absolutely. Great idea. We should have a wander around it.'

So that's exactly what we did. We picked up a map, and found picnic areas, baseball pitches, wandered down to a boating lake, and found Strawberry Fields, dedicated to the memory of John Lennon. There was nobody in the lake at this time of the morning, as it was a chilly January day. And it was so vast. Checking the map, we'd only seen a fraction of it in the three hours we'd been here. I decided that I now needed to sleep, yawning several times when Laura said, 'Car park's over that way I think, Jack?'

We walked for another half an hour before reaching the exit from the park. Then, it took a further forty minutes, taking us back past the museum, to eventually get to where we'd parked the car. We'd walked all this time holding hands. Sometimes she squeezed mine. We hardly spoke, other than to talk about directions on the map. It was a beautiful walk, tinged with the thought that it may be the only time we would ever be there. But I pushed that straight out of my mind as I held Laura tightly in my arms as we reached the car park. I turned to face her, kissing her full on the lips, holding her so tightly I could've squeezed the life out of her there and then. When our lips parted, whilst still holding each other closely she said, 'Wow, what was that for?'

'Just wanted you to know how I feel about you.'

'Jack, I've always known. I feel just the same. Now then, I think we both need a sleep, don't you?'

'Yes, boss! You're right. I'm pretty exhausted after that walk, as wonderful as it was,' I said, smiling at her.

'Same here, a bit tired myself.'

'Okay then. I'll take the front seat of the car, you want to lie down on the back seat?'

'Hmmm. Good idea. Rather lie with you, but that makes sense here,' she said, smiling briefly before continuing. 'Can you set your alarm for a couple of hours from now, on your phone? Any message from Harry yet? Then we can get back to the museum, find out where we've got to go, and who we've got to see, okay?'

'Will do. No message from Harry yet,' I replied, checking my phone.

It was almost midday, so I set my alarm for two hours from now. That'd be long enough to charge our batteries back up, I thought. Then, if we were hungry, we'd get something to eat before going inside, or even eat in there, as they'd advertised a cafe inside the museum.

Within minutes of setting the alarm on my phone, I'd fallen asleep. I could hear Laura already snoring in the back seat of the car! I didn't think that'd keep me awake. It didn't.

Next thing I knew, the alarm went off on my phone. It was still daylight. Good. I turned the alarm off, sitting back in the seat. We had time still. So, I closed my eyes and fell back into an even deeper sleep again...

***

Wriggling around in the seat, I rubbed my eyes. Oh no! The alarm had gone off, and I remembered I'd turned it off. I'd fallen back asleep! I stretched and got out of the car, feeling a bit dizzy as I quietly rubbed my face with my hands. Laura was still asleep on the back seat. It was dark in the car park. I checked my watch. I'd changed to New York time when we left the airport, so I knew the time was correct. It was past seven o'clock in the evening. No! We'd both been asleep for hours.

I turned in my seat and shook Laura gently on her shoulder.

'Laura! Wake up! Time's running out. I turned the alarm off and fell back to sleep. It's evening already. We've got to get to the museum. C'mon!'

'What? What is it, Jack?'

'Baby, I'm sorry. We both nodded off. C'mon, we've to get to the museum. It's gone seven o'clock in the evening!'

She sat up in the back of the car, rubbing her face just like me. 'I need a toilet. There's one over there by the entrance. I'll take my bag, it's in the boot with yours. Pictures of the stones are in there.'

'Okay. Toilet now, then we've got to get to the museum.'

'Right.'

I locked up the car, and Laura took the bag with the pictures and passports inside, which had a few clothes in as well. I left my bag and our case in the boot of the car. We didn't need them. We had to get a move on. I was normally cool, calm, and collected, but felt panic now, with so little time left, as we both went into the toilets.

We came out almost simultaneously.

'Hey, I knew we were tired.' She smiled after she said this. It calmed my mood instantly.

'Sorry.'

'Jack, its fine. We've time. Lucky it's open later today.'

Then she kissed me, took my hand, and we walked through the car park, out into the cold evening air, which woke me up even more.

In the distance we could see the lights of the museum. It looked fantastic. Bright lights adorned it, as day had turned into night.

Reaching the steps, we went up to the entrance to pay the fee. We didn't see the same guard—not yet anyway. Once we'd paid and got our tickets, we looked at the map inside. Ancient artefacts, shields, and stones were what we needed to track down. Laura found them on the map. They were on the first floor, where she'd said they would be after searching on the internet.

We went through a massive foyer area, where the reception was, and behind that was an enormous staircase which had various paintings adorning the walls. When we got to the top, there were several rooms with different names on them. Modern art. Roman. Paintings by the greats. Varying artefacts from all over the world.

Laura grabbed my arm, then my hand, before saying. 'There. Over there. Look.'

In the distance I could see glass cabinets, just like the ones she'd shown me on the computer at home. We held hands as we walked slowly towards the six glass cabinets.

When we got there I couldn't see at all, because there were about twenty people in front of us, obscuring our view. So we waited patiently until they walked away. They were a group, it seemed, as one of them was talking in a raised voice in a foreign language I couldn't understand. There were lots of people around. It was very busy, just like the security guard had said it would be.

After the group had gone, we had a view of the cabinets, all six of them. I couldn't see any stones which matched Mum's or the pictures we had. Laura looked at me. 'We're in the right place. I know we are. But there's no matching stone! It's not here! We'll need to ask the curator or somebody.'

I could see panic starting to set in on her face for the first time, and in her voice. So I decided to do the sensible thing and ask a member of staff.

Wandering around for a few moments, I found one. A woman dressed in a green uniform, with the logo of the Met Museum on it. She had a name tag, which showed her name; Maureen.

'Hello there.' I said, 'We're trying to find a particular stone we thought was here at the museum. It dates back to Neolithic times and is one of a group, or set of four stones, in total. They are all—we believe—from one particular stone, and are ancient artefacts. But we can't find the one stone here we're looking for. You see, we know where the other three are in Great Britain, and we're researching for our studies. We sent an email to the curator a couple of days ago, to try and see it.' I looked at her, waiting for a reply. She took her time.

'Well, you've come to the right person. I'm Maureen, and my own particular interest is ancient stones. The curator has actually briefed us about the email. Exciting for us. Now, you won't find the stone you're looking for, but I know where it is.'

'Really? We've got some photos to match up with the stones we have, we think they're cut from the same one stone, thousands of years ago.' I tried to hide the excitement and anguish in my voice as I spoke.

'Wow, that's amazing! I saw you looking at the stones and wondered if you had a real interest in them,' she replied.

'Yes, we do. A real interest.' I looked at Laura then, knowing her life depended on finding this one fourth stone, as she walked over to join our conversation.

'Would you like to follow me?' replied Maureen, 'I'll need to see some identification first, and your photos as well. This is quite an exciting find, if you really do have the other stones. Come on, I'll take you to an office where we can check the pictures.'

She took us to an office door, where she put a code into the keypad. We followed her in. She was about five feet tall, with short blond hair, though very smart in her green uniform.

'Please take a seat. My name's Maureen. Maureen Fellows. I'm sorry for appearing vague, I have a hearing problem and have to try and lip read people in the museum. Don't be offended if I seem to stare at you. I'm seeing what you say, due to my near deafness.'

'Thank you, Maureen. I'm Laura. This is, Jack. We've come to try and find one particular stone. Can we show you the three that we have pictures of?'

'Yes, please do, Laura.'

She took the pictures out of her bag, placing them on the desk in front of Maureen.

She stared at the photos. Just stared at them.

Finally, after what felt like four or five minutes of silence, but was only one, Maureen looked up from the photos.

'This is amazing! Do you know what you've got here?'

'Well, not exactly. These three pictures are ancient Irish stones. We believe that there's a fourth piece, here in your museum in New York. We've been conducting research into its whereabouts, as we've had an interest in archaeology for some time now,' Laura said, not wanting to give Maureen the whole story of what we were trying to achieve.

She was winging it, making it up as she went along. We had to be careful, still not knowing where the fourth stone was. But Maureen, I could see, was getting excited.

'It's not here on display. The stone I think you want to see was donated to the museum by an eccentric millionaire years ago. He'd got the stone from Ireland about twenty-five years ago. Said he'd bought it because of some readings in a book. The Book of Scrolls, I think it was called. He said it was one of four stones, just like you've said. It's not on display right now, like I've already said, because a few days ago, it was in one of the cabinets you were looking at. We had an incident. It started to glow! Nobody knew why. So, we had it removed.' The excitement was immense in her voice now.

'Where's it been put, Maureen? Any idea?' She didn't see my face when I spoke, so I wasn't sure she'd heard me, as she looked at the photos again, before continuing to speak. 'Mr John Rumsfield—the millionaire who donated it years ago—said that if anything ever happened to the stone, it had to be removed from public view immediately. That's exactly what we had to do a few days ago. It was very exciting. I was on duty that day, I'm only a part-time member of staff. He always believed one day something would happen to the stone. Now you've arrived! How exciting!'

'Do you know the whereabouts of the stone now, Maureen?' I said, trying to remain calm and not join in her own excitement, looking directly at her face so she could understand me.

'It's been placed in the basement of the museum. I suppose you'd call it a cellar in Britain. Anyway, six or seven days ago when the incident happened, the owner placed it under twenty-four hour guard. He's paying for it. So, we've got a twenty four hour watch on the stone. And furthermore, if anyone asks about the stone, we're to contact him immediately and say it's been removed from the building. He wanted us to lie for him. But not to you, as you're the people who contacted us via email. And you have the photos. This is quite incredible.'

'Can we see the stone, Maureen, in the basement?' asked, Laura.

'Oh, well, I see from your pictures that it'll match. Look, I've got a photo of our stone here in the drawer.'

She took out a picture of the stone and put it on the desk with the three we had. I couldn't quite believe it at first. Looking at the shards and shapes of all four of them, I could see that they'd all fit. We didn't have Mum's three stones, only pictures of them. But they matched! I could barely hold my excitement, when I blurted out to Maureen. 'Please Maureen, can you take us to see the stone? We call it the fourth stone. It'd mean a lot to us both.'

'Let me get a colleague to call Mr Rumsfield first. He doesn't live far away and we have to call him. His instructions were that if anyone asked about this stone, we had to call him immediately. You're the first people to ever ask about the stone. Apart from the man earlier today.'

'Man earlier today?' I said, slight panic now in my voice.

'Yes, nice gentleman, had a moustache. And he mouthed words like you, different to watching an American speak. I would guess he was English or British like you two.'

Dempsey. Had to be. Laura and I looked at each other. We said nothing, just stared at each other. He'd actually followed us here! He'd made it! Unbelievable.

'Maureen, could you get your colleague to call Mr Rumsfield, and maybe then arrange for us to go and see the stone?'

'Sure. The other gentleman wanted to see it too. I just told him it wasn't here anymore. He seemed agitated and not satisfied that it wasn't on display. So, I called security, who escorted him out of the museum. I told him again it wasn't here. Technically, I was telling the truth, as it's not here on display, but in the basement.'

'Is it here, Maureen, the stone?' Laura asked again.

'Yes, it is.'

'So, can you ask a colleague to call this Mr Rumsfield, please?' said Laura, almost pleading.

'I'll see what I can do. The other gentleman said when he was being escorted out of the museum, that he'd be back. So, our security team are on alert for the time being, as he was only here three or four hours ago. Unusual that you've asked about the stone on the same day as well. But, like you said, you're researching and have these amazing photos. Do you have your identification please, before I organise the call?'

'Absolutely. Jack, passports are in my bag, both of them.'

I found our passports, handing them over to Maureen. She looked at us for a few seconds and gave them straight back.

'Good. Thanks for that. I'll arrange for contact with the owner. He lives about an hour away from the museum. I think he'd like to meet you both. Now, as far as I'm concerned, you've been identified as the two people who emailed us a couple of days ago. I will explain that I'm satisfied you are who you say you are. Mr Rumsfield will accept that from me.'

'Shall we wait here?' questioned Laura.

'Yes, that'd be fine. Help yourself to water in the machine if you like, I'll be back shortly.'

'Thank you for your help. You're very kind, Maureen,' Laura said, calmer now.

'Well, like I say, I'm here to help. Be back soon.' Then she left us in the room to wait.

Ten minutes went by, and my mobile phone went off. It was a text message. From Harry. It read:

No news yet. Can't make out the other words or letters. I'll keep trying. Hope you've got to the museum by now. Harry x

Showing it to Laura, I decided to call him. The signal was good even inside the building. About a minute later, he answered my call.

'Jack, is that you?'

'Yes, Harry. No news yet about the other letters in the book?'

'Not yet. I'll call or text again to let you know. But I've got the letter "r". I can see that, and it's in two separate words, as well as the letter "n", I think.'

'Good work, Harry. Keep trying. We're in the museum. And you were right. Seems like Dempsey made it. He's been to the museum before us. He must've got a flight just after us. Security escorted him out of the museum earlier, before we got here.'

'How come he got there before you?'

'We fell asleep. Exhausted. Sat in the car and nodded off. But we're here now, and we think we know where the stone is. Problem is, it's guarded by security now.'

'Why?'

'Well, a few days ago—must've been the exact time we were at the shrine—the fourth stone started to glow. Just like the other three did. Got to be connected. The owner asked to be contacted if anything ever happened to his stone. So, he wanted it removed for safe keeping, and it's under guard now, in the basement of the museum.'

'Oh no! How're you going to get to it now?'

'We've got a woman working in the museum who's helping us. She's contacting the owner. Gone eight o'clock in the evening here, so we've got some time still, but not much. The owner is coming to see us, if this lady can get hold of him.'

'Jack, it all sounds a bit too much to take. But, how come it's open so late? Are you both all right?'

'Laura's good. I'm okay. It's a celebration of Martin Luther King tomorrow, it opens late for this one day a year. Lucky for us. Not sure where this basement is, but like I said, there's time still.'

'It'll work out, Jack. It's got to.'

'I hope so, Harry.'

There was silence on the line between us. I was getting worried now—with so little time left. Then Harry spoke again after a few seconds.

'Right, I'll crack on here and let you know when I've deciphered this page. Bye for now, Jack.'

I knew he was trying to remain confident for us.

'Great. Thanks. Speak to you soon. Bye.' Then I cut off the phone. Laura had heard the conversation, as I'd put the phone between us, so we could listen to the call together.

We sat quietly, not speaking for a few minutes.

'We're wasting time, Laura. Look, there's a map on the wall there, of the museum. C'mon, we've got to get to that basement.'

'No, Jack. Wait. I know and feel that we've got to sit tight. She'll be back soon, don't worry. Please, don't worry.'

'But, there's less than four hours before midnight here, and you've got to hold that stone in your hand, plus whatever else we've to do! It's being guarded and we're waiting for this owner to turn up! I'm worried, Laura. I don't want to lose you again.' I was getting agitated myself now.

'Jack, you'll never lose me. That's not going to happen. Stay calm. Trust me.' She smiled at me, kissing me afterwards.

Then, as our lips parted, she squeezed my hand. Almost immediately, the door to the office opened and Maureen walked back in.

'So, we've contacted Mr Rumsfield, he's on his way. But due to traffic he'll be here in about an hour or so. He's in town at a function, so that's lucky.'

'Thanks. That's good. Really appreciate your help with this, Maureen, it means a hell of a lot to us. Doesn't it, Jack?'

'Yes, thank you. Great news. Can you take us to the stone now, or shall we wait for him?' My tone was calmer now, thanks to Laura's wise words.

'We can go to the basement, I'll take you there. But we can't see the stone until he arrives,' Maureen replied.

'Okay, thanks again. Lead the way, we'll be right behind you. C'mon Jack, let's go.'

'Follow me, we've to go to the other side of the museum.'

Then, Maureen turned towards the door, letting us out before locking it behind us. We followed her through the main building, past paintings, statues, displays of Indian clothing and weapons, back down the staircase. Then, she took us to the ground floor, where we went through a small door; this one had a keypad code she used for access.

Once we'd got through this doorway, we went downstairs again via a short spiral staircase. This had to be the basement area. We were nearly there.

Finally, getting off the stairs, we were in a big, wide open corridor, which led to another door. This door was twice the size of the other doors we'd been through.

Maureen opened the door, using her shoulder as well as the handle once she'd tapped in the code into the keypad. We'd made it to the basement, and we all walked through the big metal door.

Standing in the basement, it surprisingly had a small window to one side. It was one enormous rectangular room, about the size of an enormous warehouse. In front of us, about fifty metres away, stood two security guards. Directly behind them, I could see glass cases and cabinets with all manner of armour, shields, pictures big and small, glassware, and bowls, and then I saw some stones as well. Ironic, how it felt like a giant version of Mum's parlour.

One of the guards I recognised as the guy we'd spoken to in the morning outside the museum, before we had gone back to the car and fallen asleep. They were standing in front of an area that had wooden panels all around it, that was not much bigger than an old phone box. I looked at Laura, and she did me, at the same time. We both knew this was likely to be where the fourth stone was.

'There's a table and chairs over there, if you'd like to sit for a while before Mr Rumsfield arrives shortly.'

'Thanks, Maureen,' I replied, looking straight into her eyes as I continued to say, 'and behind the wooden panels, is that where the stone is?'

'It is. But, you'll have to wait until he arrives. He knows you're here, and wants to talk to you about why and how you've turned up, especially after the other chap arrived today as well.'

'That's fine. Thank you, Maureen. Are you waiting with us now?' asked Laura.

'No, I've to wait for him at the front of the museum. Even Mr Rumsfield doesn't have access here, though it's his property we're guarding. Only staff with passes and code access are allowed in—like myself. I'll be back with him in a while, hopefully within the hour. Then you can tell him your story, about the pictures of the stones you have back in England. I told him, via my colleague, that they matched his stone. I think he'll be very excited when he arrives to talk to you.'

Then she left through the big heavy door, with the help of a guard closing it after her.

We sat at the table for a few minutes until Laura got up. She walked over to the guard we'd spoken to outside, earlier in the day.

'So, how long have you worked at the museum, er, Ralph?'

I saw her look to his security badge before she spoke, to see his name. He was a big man. So I decided to walk over and join her.

'Ma'am, I'm not supposed to say. But seeing as y'all seem decent folks from England I've no gumption in talking to you both.'

'Thanks, Ralph. That's decent of you. Jack here, and myself, have come to look at a particular stone. Amazingly it's the one you're looking after.'

'Well ma'am, nobody's allowed into this makeshift booth. Orders of the owner, I've been told. So, I'm not at liberty to let you in without his permission.'

'I quite understand. We'll take a seat and wait for them to return. Thanks again.'

Laura and I turned away from the two security guards, returning to the seats at the table again. Sitting down, Laura took the pictures out of her bag, along with a bottle of water.

'Jack, we've got that guard on our side if anything happens. Even chatting to him, he's opened up to us, knowing that we're honest people. I'm going back to show him the photos we've got, see if he's seen the fourth stone inside the booth. It'll confirm what Maureen has already said. Then we know we're one hundred percent in the right place. Somehow we've to convince this Mr Rumsfield to let us see it, and then to let me hold it, with whatever else we've to do.'

'Okay then. I'll sit and have a drink of water, you take the photos over to both of the guards and ask. D'you feel comfortable about this? I know you've got stronger instincts since you came back?'

'Yes, I do. I'll bat my eyelids or something like that if I need to.'

We both laughed quietly to ourselves, before she got up and walked over to the guards a second time.

'D'you mind if I ask you to have a look at these photos, Ralph?'

'Sure, ma'am. No objection in looking. What've you got there?'

'Well, the fourth stone—the one inside this booth as we call it—we believe is part of one big stone. These three photos are of the other stones we have in England. And we're hoping that this makes up the one stone that is possibly sacred and could have been used thousands of years ago in sacrificial rituals. At least that's what we're hoping, Ralph.'

'Real interesting, ma'am. Your photos look just like the one in there. Same colour, too. Won't be long before you can check properly.'

'Thanks for looking at the photos. Could I just ask what happened a few days ago, when the stone was removed from the cabinet? Were you on duty?'

'Hmm. I was. Lot of commotion that day, 'bout a week ago. Maureen was on duty too. She got real excited. It was me who called the owner. We had to evacuate the floor the stone was on. Y'know, it started to glow green. Real peculiar. Never seen anything like it, ever!'

'And what happened when Mr Rumsfield arrived?'

As I watched Laura talking to the security guard named Ralph, I could see his eyes open wider, as if excited, as he continued to talk to her.

'Well, don't know I should be telling y'all. But anyways, he came bounding up to the first floor where the stone was; fortunate he was in town. Had his own key for his cabinet. Told everyone to stand back. He opened it while the stone was still glowing. Turned round and told me—I was standing right there guarding it—to escort him to the basement.'

'Wow! And what did you do next?'

'When we got here, a glass cabinet—inside these panels—was already in place to put the stone in. He had it in his hand, inside a hanky or napkin. Didn't want to touch the stone himself. And wanted nobody else to touch it either.'

'So, you had a kind of security alert inside the building?'

'Not so much an alert as a lot of excitement. Today, it's more like an alert; especially after the other guy was escorted out of the museum a few hours ago.'

'Thanks for looking at the photos, Ralph. I'll pop back to my seat and wait again.'

'No problem. Looks like you've got a match with the stones.'

I was still sitting on the chair when Laura walked back over to me after finishing showing the guard the photos. She'd got more information than we'd hoped for. But we'd temporarily forgotten about Dempsey until she sat down again. The guard had just reminded us both that he was here. While we waited for Maureen and Mr Rumsfield to arrive, we sat silently, hoping not to see Laura's father again today.

20. Dempsey's confrontation.

We sat and waited for quite some time. Well over three hours. Maureen had popped back once to say Mr Rumsfield had been delayed and wouldn't be with us until past eleven p.m., when the museum would be closed. But she assured us he'd be coming this evening and that permission to allow us to wait had been given. Finally, a little past eleven thirty p.m.—with both of us glancing at each other, getting very concerned about running out of time—the big metal door finally opened.

In walked Maureen. Behind her was a man we didn't know. It had to be Mr Rumsfield. He was short, about five feet six inches in height, bald, and wearing a dark blue suit with one of those watches on a chain hanging from his waistcoat. He didn't look happy.

In the next moment, we knew why he wasn't happy. Directly behind him was Dempsey!

Laura and I jumped out of our chairs in shock, taking a few steps backwards away from the table. I didn't expect to see him now, even though he'd made it here to New York. But worse was to come. As he walked in directly behind Rumsfield, turning into the basement from the doorway, we saw why the owner of the stone was so unhappy. Dempsey had a gun pointed in his back!

When they'd all got into the basement, Dempsey closed the door behind himself, then looked straight over to us.

'Hello, Jack. See you've got my daughter with you. Told you this wouldn't work, didn't I?'

'You idiot! D'you know what you're doing? You don't get it, do you?' I shouted at him.

'Both of you stay exactly where you are. Don't move,' he shouted at the two guards in front of the booth where the fourth stone was, pointing the gun directly at them. They froze, not daring to move a muscle. They'd both seen him waving the gun around.

He walked towards us, with the gun turned again into the back of Rumsfield, pushing Maureen forward with his free hand. All three of them came to us, and Dempsey pushed Maureen down into a chair. He looked her in the eye, put his finger in front of his mouth, signalling to her not to talk. I could see real fear in her eyes. Then, in an instant, he looked back at Laura and I, still holding the gun to Rumsfield's back.

'Jack. I know exactly what I'm doing. Stopping evil being unleashed by allowing my daughter to die, as harsh as that sounds. You should've let her go when she went the first time. I told you, it's you who's responsible for all of this! I wish I'd never been persuaded by you and your family. Well, now it's over, for you as well!' I saw hatred towards me in his eyes, and he literally spat the words out at me.

As soon as he spoke, I knew he was going to kill me. That way, I would be with Laura, in his mind at least, even if she walked the earth as a spirit. I had to think fast, but I wasn't fast enough. Laura spoke before me.

'Dad. Why? It didn't have to come to this!'

She was pleading with him. I saw tears in her eyes. Then I heard my phone ring. I grabbed for it in my pocket.

'Don't answer that!' Dempsey shouted.

'But it's Harry. Look. See, it's his name!' I shouted back at Dempsey.

'Make it your last call. Make it quick, Jack. Time to depart now. Say goodbye, I'll let you at least do that. Where I go doesn't matter afterwards. Answer it!'

'Harry?'

'Yes, Jack. You okay?'

'No, not really. We're inside the museum, Dempsey's here too. Looks like we're not going to make it after all, Harry. Sorry.' I knew my voice was wavering with emotion; it was difficult to control myself now.

'Don't give up, Jack! I've got it! I translated the words. It says "held in your arms". When Laura gets the stone—if she gets it—you have to hold her in your arms, but in moonlight! Just like you told me you'd held her when she passed over. But you've got to be in moonlight, somehow!'

'Oh, Harry. Now I know, but it's too late.' I replied, feeling like a man beaten, falling at the last hurdle of a race when winning.

'No Jack, don't let it be!'

Dempsey moved away from behind Rumsfield then, taking big strides towards me, yanking the phone from my hand.

'Goodbye, Harry. Say cheerio to your mum for us!' he shouted into the phone.

Then he turned the phone off as he went back to Rumsfield, dropping it on the floor, stamping on it wildly. His rage was immense. As he smashed his foot down several times, his face reddened with anger, and the phone began to fall apart into pieces.

As he did this, Rumsfield took his chance to grab the gun from Dempsey.

I saw him turn to face Dempsey, grabbing at his hand holding the gun. Dempsey quickly realised what was happening as the pair of them fell to the ground. He took a punch from the stone owner, but then we heard a shot. The gun had gone off. There was an eerie silence for a few moments, and nobody moved.

Dempsey had shot Rumsfield!

As they lay on the ground, rolling over each other, we could see a trickle of blood coming from between them. Laura stared at her father, open-mouthed. He'd shot Rumsfield! A man who could've helped us.

'What the hell have you done, Dad!?'

Dempsey got up and took a step away from the body on the floor, as Laura went to help Mr Rumsfield. She dropped to the floor, cradling the head of the man she barely knew. Rumsfield looked up at Laura as she leant over him, and I joined her, dropping to my knees. He smiled at her. His eyes averted, down towards his waist. In his hand, lying underneath his body, he held his watch. Laura held the watch briefly for a moment so that I could see that the bullet had glanced off it. Although it'd hit him, he'd only had a glancing blow, though he was bleeding. It seemed that he was going to be all right.

I nodded to Laura and whispered, 'Harry told me what to do. I know. Mr Rumsfield, just lie there as if you're unconscious. Please. We'll explain everything to you soon.'

Laura nodded back.

Rumsfield winked at me as well. There was no time to explain, I thought. I had to act fast.

'You've killed him, Dempsey. You'll go to prison for this!' I shouted.

'No I won't! You're going to hell!'

As I lunged at him, he aimed the gun at me and fired. Maureen was right next to him, grappling for the gun. But I felt no pain from the bullet. Nothing. Just an enormous bang.

Instead I felt my body hitting him full on, tackling him as he fell backwards, over the table where Maureen had been sitting moments ago.

I was on top of him as we both fell off the table. In an instant I clambered to my feet. Dempsey lay on the floor still. He had blood all over his chest.

Was it my blood? I checked my clothes. Hardly any blood. I was standing upright, apparently unmarked by a bullet, but I didn't know how.

I could see Dempsey was now writhing in agony on the floor.

Glancing away from him, I could see the two guards were now racing over to help Laura, who was still on the floor with Mr Rumsfield.

Then I saw Maureen. She was standing just a few feet away from me. She had the gun in her hand.

'What happened, Maureen?' I said, not looking at her face.

She didn't hear me. I wasn't looking at her. She needed to see my face to read my lips. I remembered she was deaf.

I put my hands on her arms and looked into her face.

'Maureen? Maureen? It's me, Jack. Look at me. Please!'

'Yes, Jack. What is it?'

'What did you do?'

'Er. Er.'

'It's all right Maureen. It's okay. Just tell me slowly.'

She stared at me for a few seconds and I could hear Dempsey's moans and groans, as he lay on the ground.

'He was pointing the gun at you. I got out of my chair and grabbed his arm as you lunged at him. It turned in towards his body. I didn't let go. I held on tightly to him. Then I felt his whole body jerk away when you dived at him. Now I've got the gun in my hand.'

I glanced around and saw Rumsfield on the floor still. Both of the guards were with him. The one we knew as Ralph was holding him up in a seated position. He was going to be okay, I hoped, with his pocket watch maybe having saved his life.

Turning towards Dempsey, I saw Laura had gone over to him in the commotion, holding his head in her arms. Blood was all over his chest and upper body.

'It's all going to be all right,' I said to Maureen, looking into her eyes. 'Just sit down here. You've been amazingly brave. I'll take the gun from you. It's okay.'

I sat her on one of the chairs at the table. She nodded, then sat down. She was in shock, I thought. But I think she'd saved my life.

Rushing over to Laura, I put the gun in my pocket. She was holding her Dad in her arms now. He was dying. Really dying.

'Laura. I'm sorry. I've been a fool. Please forgive me.' Dempsey said, struggling to say the words.

She stared at her father as he whispered the words and nodded. She didn't speak. She couldn't.

He was taking his last breath on Earth as I got to his other side. He was gasping for breath, but that wouldn't help him now, as I saw his chest was covered in his own blood.

'I can see her, Laura. It's her. She's waiting for me.'

'Oh, Dad,' Laura said quietly to him, crying as her Dad drifted away with a small smile on his lips. He'd paid the ultimate price. He needn't have died this way, I thought. But I never said that to Laura. I think she already knew.

We held him together in our arms for a few moments before Laura looked up at me. What could I say to her? Her own father had just died in her arms.

'Jack? This is madness,' she said in a whisper, with tears rolling down her cheeks.

'I'm sorry. So sorry,' was all I could say. No words would help now.

We gently laid her father on the floor of the basement, and Laura let his head drop from her arms.

Dempsey was dead.

I looked up, above Laura, to see the clock on the basement wall. It was 11.47 now.

Time had flown quicker than we'd realised. My brain came back to me. I knew that time was running out fast. 'Listen, we've only got a few minutes left.'

'It's no use, Jack. I know you said earlier you'd know what to do. We've survived this far, but Harry never got the chance to tell you what else to do, did he, other than holding the stone?'

Her eyes lit up, before she spoke again. 'Did you say he told you? Did he tell you?'

I nodded. 'Yes. He did. Come on. Not much time left now. We need someone to help us. And quickly.'

Looking over at the guards and Rumsfield, then glancing back at Maureen, I knew exactly what I had to do now.

21. Maureen helps out.

Looking back at Dempsey's body, I helped Laura off the ground. As tragic as this was, there really was nothing more we could do for him now.

We walked to Maureen, who was still sitting on one of the chairs at the table. She was staring into nothingness, in shock.

'Hey, Maureen. You've been incredibly brave here. But we'd like a little more help, if you can. Please?' I said, looking again directly into her face and eyes.

'Jack. What's going on here? That man's been shot. I think he's dead. And poor old Mr Rumsfield's been shot too.'

'I know. Now, look at me and listen, Maureen. Please. One day, I'll explain everything to you. Laura and I will tell you everything. Now, we've got very little time left. Thank you for saving my life. That will never be forgotten. But, please, we need your help one more time.'

She didn't speak for a few moments, still in shock from what had just happened.

'Something tells me you're good people. Er, what can I do?'

Laura came and stood next to me, to speak to Maureen herself.

'Well, Maureen. Jack and I need to get to that fourth stone in the small booth. We need to get Rumsfield and the two guards out of here. He's been shot, so needs an ambulance to get him to hospital.'

As she stared at Laura, Maureen' eyes became more alert.

'What do I need to do?' she said, suddenly realising the importance of the situation, as Laura held her hands.

I glanced over to Rumsfield. The two guards were helping him to his feet. Then Laura spoke again.

'Like I said, we need to get the guards and Rumsfield out of here. Right now. Then we don't want anyone in here for a few minutes. Jack and I have to see the stone. Alone.'

She looked at me. Then glanced back at Laura. There was an eerie silence for a few seconds before Laura spoke again.

'I'm sorry, we really can't say why right now. It's nearly midnight and we truly haven't got time, Maureen. Please, trust us. One day, if I make it through this, I will personally explain to you—just you—what this is all about. I promise.'

There was a silence between all three of us again. We waited for a minute, while she decided whether to help us or not.

Finally, Maureen broke the silence.

'Okay you two. Leave it to me.'

'Let me help you up, Maureen,' I said, as she was still sitting in the chair.

'I'm fine, Jack, thank you,' she said, getting up from the chair herself unaided. 'Now, I'll get rid of them, then I'll guard the door myself. I can give you about five minutes. That's all. By then, the NYPD will be swarming all over this place. They're outside the building already, after *he* came in with the gun and grabbed Mr Rumsfield and myself,' she continued, pointing to Dempsey lying dead on the floor a few feet away from us.

'Thank you. If we make it, Jack and I will never forget this,' Laura replied.

'Leave it to me. Five minutes, mind?'

'Okay, Maureen,' said, Laura.

Then, she turned and walked over to the others. She stood in front of them for a few seconds before speaking again.

'Right. Listen. Here's the thing. We've got to get out of here. Now! All of us. C'mon. Mr Rumsfield, let's get you out to a paramedic, and hospital. I'm setting the alarm off as soon as we're outside the door.'

'Okay, let's go. You two over there, you following us out?' shouted Ralph the security guard.

'Yes, Ralph. Be right behind you,' I said, knowing we were staying with Dempsey's body.

'Come on. Now!' Maureen shouted at the two guards, with real authority in her voice. 'The alarm's outside the door. Mr Rumsfield, can you walk with the guard's help?'

'Yes. Thanks, Maureen.' He sounded weak. He'd lost some blood, but seemed like he'd hopefully survive his wound.

When they walked to the door, Maureen punched in the code and Ralph opened it with a big strong hand, then he walked out with the other guard, holding Rumsfield between them, as Maureen followed them out. She was the last one to go through the door, turning to us as it closed. I heard her shout, 'Five minutes. Alarm going off now!'

That was our cue. And it sounded like the door had locked itself automatically after she'd set the alarm off.

She'd done what she said she would. The clock said seven minutes to midnight as I glanced up to it, and Laura spoke.

'See the time?'

'I know.'

'C'mon. Let's get to the stone. What did Harry tell you?'

'No time. Hurry up, I'll explain on the way.'

22. The fourth stone.

With the door closed and Maureen having set the alarm off, we were trapped inside the basement. Alone. With Dempsey's body. Just over five minutes left to bring Laura back. That's all we had now, after everything we'd been through.

'You ready, Laura?'

'I'm fine. Let's get into that booth to get the stone.'

We walked quickly from near Dempsey's body, after hearing the door slam shut and the alarm siren starting, making our way across the room to the booth where the stone was kept. Laura stopped to stare at her father's body for a moment, glancing at me after she did so. I put my arm around her.

'Come on,' I whispered, and nodded at her, turning her away from his dead, bloodied body.

We made our way to the panelled booth of wood. There was no lock on the door at all. Walking inside, we saw a glass cabinet. There, inside, we saw it for the first time.

It was the fourth stone.

We gaped at it. It wasn't glowing green now, but it was the right stone, I could tell by the shape.

'Listen. Harry told me what to do. We know you've got to hold the stone in your hands. But there's more than just that, to bring you back for good.'

'No time for puzzles, Jack! Come on. What else. There's five minutes left. I don't want to leave you— again!'

'Sorry. Not meaning to play games. Just thinking about what he said before Dempsey grabbed the phone off me and smashed it.'

'What did Harry say?'

'You've got to hold the stone, Laura.'

'I know that, Jack! What else?' she said, with desperation in her voice.

'He said "held in your arms", meaning I've to hold you in my arms. Just like I did that day at the train station, when you... '

'I know. I know. Okay. Let's get the stone out of the cabinet. Now, Jack! I'm feeling faint.'

Looking at Laura, I could see she was going pale again. I glanced up at the clock again, checking my own watch. Four minutes till midnight. That's all we had. Panic took over my body momentarily.

'Right. Stand back.'

I smashed the glass cabinet with my fist. It was the quickest way to get the stone out into her hands. Instantly I had blood on my hand and arm, but the glass was smashed into pieces, enough for me to grab the stone from inside.

'Your hand and arm, Jack!'

'It's fine. C'mon, there's no time to bother about that now.'

Picking the stone up with my bloodied hand and arm, with shards of glass in it, I passed it to Laura quickly. She held the fourth stone tightly with her hands cupped around it. It started to glow green. We stared at each other, and a flicker of a smile came onto her face. I just hoped it'd work.

'Let's get out of this booth, Jack. I feel like I'm going to collapse. I'm dizzy. What's happening to me?'

She stopped smiling and started to cry. I could see she was fading fast. The outline of her whole face was transparent. No time left, almost. I picked her up while she held the glowing stone in her hands, putting my arms under her legs and around her back, cradling her tightly, just like at the train station. I ignored the pain in my arm from the glass. I felt faint myself now. *This should do it*, I thought, as I walked out of the booth.

'Jack, it's not working! What's wrong?'

I stood inside the basement now, holding her in my arms. She was fading away. Why? I looked at the clock on the wall again. Two minutes to midnight.

'Jack. What else did he say to you?'

'Held in your arms. Held in your arms. That's it. Oh God, think!' I shouted at myself, trying to get my fading brain to remember.

'Jack. It's all right. Thank you for everything. For even trying. We got to see America briefly, didn't we? I love you.'

There was now only a minute until midnight, when I remembered.

'Moonlight! Held in your arms in moonlight!'

***

264

I looked over to the small window. I could see a beam of light flashing through it, directed at the big entrance door. It was shining off the metal. It was the slither of moonlight we needed.

Knowing I had seconds to get there, I could feel the searing pain in my arm as I held Laura. It was stinging and hurt like hell. I knew I'd lost some blood when I smashed the glass to get the fourth stone, but had no idea how much. No time to think about that now.

Holding her tightly, I raced towards the entrance door. I could feel myself slipping away into unconsciousness, with the blood I was losing right now.

'Laura, I... I... ,' my vision was fading. I felt dizzy. Then I heard her voice one last time.

'Jack! Keep going, don't give up. Hold me! Tightly! We're going to make it!'

I saw the moonlight, and fell towards it; it bathed us and I still held Laura cradling her in my arms. The light covered us for a few seconds. I said to her, as I dropped to the ground with my back against the door, 'Have we made it, Laura? Have we?' She didn't answer me. I didn't hear her reply. I'd failed. It was all my fault. It was over. Everything went black. Pure darkness.

23. Waking up.

The next thing I knew, I was waking up in an ambulance. There was no sign of Laura as I opened my eyes, trying to look around. I wasn't sure where I was, or even if I was dead or alive.

'Hey mister, you back with us? Thought we'd lost you there for a while,' said a paramedic, leaning over me. I couldn't see properly, but it looked like I had a drip in my arm.

'Er. Where am I? Where's Laura?'

'Settle down, buddy, we're on the way to hospital. You've lost a lot of blood, but now you're with us again, so just stay with us okay?'

'But where's Laura!?'

'Take it easy. Take it easy. Just rest a while. There's no one named Laura here with us. I'll ask when we get to the hospital.'

Thinking I'd lost her, I slipped back into unconsciousness, thinking she'd gone for good and I'd failed after everything we'd gone through these past two weeks.

***

Later, I came to in hospital. At least, I thought it was a hospital, as it was white and bright, with people rushing around in white coats. I could feel severe pain in my left arm, remembering how I had smashed the glass cabinet before carrying Laura to the door, holding her and trying to get to the moonlight. I was alive! But she wasn't here now.

I thought it'd been a waste of time. Everything we'd done. All the things we'd been through in the last two weeks. Wasted. I began crying to myself in my bed. No nurses came, no doctors. I was alone. I thought I'd failed to save her, the one true love of my life. I fell back to sleep again.

When I woke up later, I'd no idea how long I'd been asleep for. I felt groggy, and I saw a nurse come to my bedside.

'Excuse me, nurse, could you tell me how long I've been here?'

'You take it easy, Jack. You're a bit of a celebrity around these parts y'know?'

'What? How d'you know my name? I just want to know how long I've been here. Please?'

'Four days. Lots of commotion about you locally, here in Manhattan. Got some lady friends who want to talk to you. You feel up to talking to them?'

'Laura? Did she make it?'

She smiled at me before continuing, 'Well, there's a lady here named Connie who's been waiting two days to see you. And another lady, too, Maureen. She's been outside here for three days. D'you want to see them?'

'I s'pose so. Thank you, nurse.' I felt deflated. I knew who they both were, but why had they come to see me? It'd been a waste of time, I thought. I was without Laura now.

'Had to get you identified, there have been pictures on the television. Connie recognised you. She'd like to just make sure you're okay. And Maureen—she's the lady who says she saved your life?' the nurse said.

'That's true. I'd like to see them. Thanks.' But as the nurse turned to walk away, I continued to feel the pain in my arm, knowing that it wasn't Laura I'd see. I thought I'd just made it to the moonlight. But now, I wasn't so sure.

A few minutes went by, then the same nurse returned. She was alone. I remembered what Connie looked like from our visit to the café, and Maureen I knew from the museum. My memory was okay still, and the nurse was allowing them both in to see me. I waited, hoping against hope that I'd see someone else too.

Instead, when the nurse returned, she came up to me and whispered quietly into my ear, 'Mr Stanton, there's another lady here who wants to see you. Says she's the future Mrs Stanton. Says you saved her life.'

I stared at the nurse in disbelief. Could it be?

'Laura?'

The nurse smiled at me, nodding. Then waved a lady over to me whose face I couldn't see.

Staring at the lady approaching, I could see who it was as she got closer. *Miracles do happen*, I thought to myself. Knowing I had the biggest grin and smile on my face any man could possibly ever have, with tears welling up in my eyes, I saw her.

It was her. Laura. We'd made it.

I began to weep more as she reached me, uncontrollably. My whole body was shaking with emotion and relief. She had her colour back. Her beautiful jet black hair and green eyes looked radiant. And she smiled at me. That smile. Always for me.

'Hey, you. Mr Stanton. Got a couple of friends here with me to say hi.'

I couldn't speak at first, as I was crying so much. Seeing her after thinking I'd failed was unbelievable.

Laura leant forward and kissed me gently on the lips as I pushed myself up in my bed, still feeling weak.

'You're the one looking pale now, Jack. But not for long, huh? I'll get the colour back into your cheeks. Isn't that right Connie?' Laura said, putting her hand on my forehead, glancing back towards another lady, who I recognised as Connie.

I saw her, our waitress, standing behind Laura. I was now open-mouthed, speechless. I wiped the tears from my eyes as I gained my composure.

'Well, Jack, you'll get that colour back soon, big strong guy like you.' Said Connie, continuing, 'Saw your picture on the box. Said nobody knew who you were, other than being a guy named Jack. I knew it was you. Knew you'd need me to help identify you. And Laura, too. So when I saw you on TV a couple of days ago, I came right over. You're a good guy, Jack. Glad you made it, whatever *it* really was.'

Laura was sitting on the bed, smiling.

'Connie, thanks for identifying him. I was unconscious for three days myself after the incident at the museum, until only yesterday. The nurse said I'd been on a drip to give me fluids. Sort of brought me back to life, hey, Jack?'

'Sort of did, by the sound of it,' I said, finally starting to get my own emotions a bit more under control. 'And Maureen. Where is she? The nurse told me that she's here. I wanted to thank her.'

Just then, I saw her approaching the end of the bed. I put my right hand up to wave her towards me on the other side of the bed. When she reached me, I looked into her face and eyes and mouthed the words I knew she'd understand, but wouldn't hear.

'Maureen. We'll never be able to thank you properly for giving us five minutes in that basement. Thank you, so, so much, for everything, forever.'

She leant over and whispered to me, 'It was a pleasure, Jack. I've had a chat with Laura. I know. Your secret's safe with me. And Mr Rumsfield and the guards are all fine. I told them that I'd not heard you when I'd set the alarm off; that's why you got locked in by mistake for those five minutes. They think I'm daft for locking you in, but a heroine for what I did, as well.'

'You are in my book. You're a heroine, Maureen,' I said so that they'd all hear me.

They stood quietly around my bedside for a few moments. Until Laura spoke again.

'After being on the local news station, people finding out who you are, Jack—and me too—we've little choice but to make our home here now. Among new friends, don't you think?' she said, winking at me.

We might've got away with it, I thought, before saying, 'Sounds like a good deal to me.'

As I said this, Connie and Maureen both leant over, to kiss me on either cheek.

'Time for me to go, Jack Stanton,' said Connie. 'Don't forget to come into the cafe when you're both passing. I'll see you both again, you can count on that.'

'We shall, Connie. Thank you so much for coming to identify us. And for helping us to find our way. I've got your number, so we'll be in touch,' Laura said.

They hugged each other, then Connie blew a kiss to me as well, before turning to leave my bedside.

'And I'm going too,' said Maureen. 'They allowed me a few days off from the museum, Jack. Everything's okay, Laura's explained it all. Police report exonerates both of you from any blame. I've told them Mr Dempsey was a crazed man, possessed by anger at you taking his daughter away from England, and his death was an accident, with me stopping him from shooting you. As you say in your country, "Mum's the word". The reports are all confidential, too, so nobody other than those you tell back in England will know exactly what happened. With your own history of antiquities and your business helping to explain why you were here at all, Mr Rumsfield has made sure it stays under wraps, with his contacts here in the police hierarchy. He's got lots of people in high up places. As well as being eccentric, he's very influential. He doesn't want any bad press about the museum. But he knows, Jack. He had to.'

She leant over me a second time, looked me in the eye and said quietly, 'Goodbye for now, Jack. I'm sure we'll all meet again.' Then she turned and walked round the bed to Laura, and hugged her tightly, then walked out of the hospital, leaving Laura and I alone together for the first time in four days.

I looked at Laura, raising my eyebrows, waiting for her to speak, but said to her before she spoke, 'Mum? Harry? You been in touch yet?'

She leant towards me, close to my face so she could whisper to me. 'I've told them about Dad, Jack. Called Harry when I awoke yesterday evening and I spoke to your mum. I've had a visit from Mr Rumsfield as well. He knows the truth, like Maureen said. No choice but to tell him. Once the dust has settled, I've told him he can come and meet your mum and see the other stones. He knows the story's true, about what we've done here. He'd always believed it was possible.'

She stopped to pause for breath and to wipe her tear-stained eyes. Her efficiency was back again. There'd be a heavy price to pay for all of this, I thought, before she continued, 'The shop's been sorted with Richard's help, too. Funds are being transferred to your mum, and then she'll transfer the money when we get an account opened at a bank here.'

'And are Mum and Harry okay, after you spoke to them?'

'Good. Since the day we lost, er, lost Dad, she's been fine and feeling much better, since four days ago. No more changes since then.'

I knew what she meant. No more ageing. I just nodded, as she paused, gathering her emotions.

'And Harry's going back to Ireland in a few days, once your mum is feeling better, which she is, daily, he said. And he knows we're fine. He's waiting for us to contact him. To let us know where we are, so he and your—our—Mum can visit.'

I smiled at her, thinking to myself that she'd taken on some of Mum's characteristics; softened, even. And now, she referred to my mum as Mum and not Mother for the first time ever. Sensing what I was thinking, she said, 'Well, she is going to be my mum now, isn't she?'

'Is she now? Don't think the wedding planned is going to happen now. We're not in England any more, and likely won't be for some time, if ever. So, it's a New York wedding for us whenever I'm out of here, don't you think?'

'Play your cards right Jack, and we'll have everything we've dreamed of now. Here.'

'I agree.'

She was still sitting on the side of my bed now. I had the drip in my arm, keeping my fluid levels up. We looked into each other's eyes, both smiling. Then we kissed. We'd not kissed for four days. I always did, and always would, love kissing her. As our lips parted, I said to her, 'Got you now, Laura Dempsey.'

'And I've got forever with you, Jack Stanton.'

24. The last two years.

After finally getting out of hospital, two weeks after the incident, there was some press speculation, which was hushed up quickly by one person. That person was Mr John Rumsfield, who, three months later, invited us round to his palatial home.

In the meantime, Laura had arranged for the burial of her father. When I'd got out of hospital, we had a memorial service for him, just us, attending on our own.

We'd already received the money from Richard Leonard for the shop back in England via Mum, and had set up our own small business in New York, not far from the Metropolitan Museum. We decided to call it *The New York Curiosity Shop*. Surprisingly, no one had taken the name before.

Laura had found a nice apartment for us on the edge of Manhattan, in an area called Queens, which was predominantly Irish, so we both felt at ease and at home there, away from the hive of activity. One thing we had kept, and had pride of place, was the Belleek bowl I'd purchased all those years ago from *The Old Curiosity Shop*, when we'd first met and said hello. It was kept in a display cabinet now, in our apartment.

Meeting John Rumsfield was wonderful. He was massively into antiques, and within months had become a regular visitor to our shop, and a good friend, too, helping us to obtain visas so that we had no need to return to the UK.

We had a thriving business within a year. And we needed staff. We had the ideal people to ask. Connie worked for us now, as did Maureen, part-time. It was our way of saying thank you to them both. They had both become very good friends of ours.

And six months after it all happened, my brother Harry and Mum visited and stayed for a month. Mum hit it off with John Rumsfield instantly, and they've remained good friends to this day.

Harry was a fully-fledged priest. And when they visited, we got married. Harry took the service, like we'd originally planned, but in New York, in a small chapel. He decided to transfer to a church in Manhattan himself, to stay for good. And we didn't need to change our names, thanks to the assistance and intervention of John Rumsfield. We finally became Mr and Mrs Stanton.

Mum had aged, as we knew she would. And we asked her to stay with us. Laura had already told me she would agree, and Mum did, moving lock, stock, and barrel, bringing everything from the cottage she wanted. She wasn't sad to leave it behind after all these years, either. She still had a strong lease for life and adventure.

But she did tell a certain someone about what happened, after we'd discussed it with her. We all agreed he had a right to know the full story. That person was Richard Leonard, who'd become one of our closest friends. In fact, he has visited twice over the last couple of years and had vowed—and we believe him—never to tell anyone. Who would believe it, anyway?

Then six months ago, we had a baby. It was a girl. We don't know yet whether she'll have the compassion or intuition of Mum or Laura. Or if history was likely to repeat itself. We'd need seven children for that to happen!

There was only one name we could call our daughter. That was Maureen. Without her, I wouldn't have been here to tell the story.

So, today, just over two years after it all happened, we're off to Central Park, near where we live now, for a picnic with one of our best friends, Maureen. She also happens to be—along with Harry—a godparent to our daughter, Maureen's namesake. We call her little Mo.

Sometimes you never know what's going to happen in life. But fate had brought us here. We knew that, and it was where we were meant to be. After what we'd been through, I hoped for a nice life. Right now, we have that. Laura knew, as she told me, on a warm April morning in 2016, that it didn't matter where you were. It was about being together, she said, with the ones you love. For as long as you possibly can.